BASIC CHEMISTRY

LOVE 101 - WILLOW BAY NOVELLA

HARLOW LAYNE

BASIC CHEMISTRY

Join Harlow's mailing list to be the first to know of new releases, free books, sales, and other giveaways!

https://harlowlayne.com/newsletter/

The Big Bang isn't just a theory. I felt it the moment I laid eyes on her.

Her ruby red lips and lush curves called to me on a primal level, and I instantly knew I would do anything for her to be mine.

And then she walked into my College AP Chemistry class and introduced herself as the teacher.

Never one to back down from a challenge, I decide to get creative. Looks like I'm going to need some extra tutoring after class.

Now it's just a waiting game on how long it will take to get her out from behind the desk and into my bed.

BASIC CHEMISTRY by Harlow Layne

1

AUGUST

"Here," Walker thrusts a paper cup into my hand as he walks past me on the sidewalk.

"There better be coffee in this," I shout over my shoulder.

His only response is to flip me off before he ducks inside the music building. I give him shit, but I know he won't be around for much longer. There's been a representative from Titan Records sniffing around him and his band, Crimson Heat, for the last couple of months, and soon he'll be gone making the music he loves.

Flipping open the lid, I inhale the aroma of coffee and then take a long sip even though it burns going down. The asshole probably asked for it to be extra hot, knowing I'd drink half of it in one go, but I don't care. If I could, I'd mainline coffee into my system. It's my senior year of college, and I already know there's going to be countless all-nighters if I want to graduate with honors.

The company I've interned at the last two summers is giving

me a hefty bonus if I graduate with honors, and I'll do whatever it takes to start my professional career off right.

I finish the last of my coffee as I step inside my chemical process design class and stop dead in my tracks when I spot the best and most luscious ass directed right at me. She's bent over, going through a bag on the floor, letting her tight skirt showcase what I'm sure is her best asset. That is until she stands up and I get a look at the rest of her body.

She's all curves and sexy as sin. Everything about her oozes sex appeal, from the fabric of her shirt that's straining from her large breasts to the way her hips look like they're made for my hands to grab onto as I take her from behind. Her long brown hair curls and frames her flawless face, but what really stands out is her bright red lipstick.

Fuck, I can't help but imagine her down on her knees in front of me, sucking my cock and leaving red rings all along my shaft.

Damn. I'm going to have to thank the professor for giving us such a fine as hell TA.

Normally I'm the type of guy who sits in the back of the class, but not today. Not now. No, I'm going to be up front and center so I can get a better look at her.

I sit directly in front of the teacher's desk, hoping that the TA will do some more bending and maybe sit on the edge of the desk, so I can fantasize about fucking her on it.

Pulling out my phone, I shoot off a quick text to Walker.

Merrick: Thanks for the coffee asshole.

I almost got a second-degree burn on my tongue.

IMMEDIATELY THREE BUBBLES POP UP, AND THEN HE SENDS me the middle finger emoji. I can only laugh.

I scroll through Instagram for a minute but don't see anything that catches my eye quite like the woman in front of me. I can't stop glancing up at her and wishing for the first time in my life for a class to start early just so I can hear her voice.

The woman leans over again, but unfortunately for me, not in my direction. When she stands up, she's donning a pair of red-rimmed glasses that match the shade of her lipstick.

Holy fucking shit, she's a wet dream come true.

She looks down at her watch and then to the class at large. It's not a large class since it's specialized, but there's only one seat left open.

She moves to stand in front of the desk with her hands behind her back, accentuating a rack that I can only imagine is at least triple D. What I wouldn't give for the sprinkler system to turn on and soak that white shirt of hers.

"Good morning, class. This is Chemical Process Design. If you're not supposed to be in here, now's the time to leave." She gives everyone a moment, and when no one leaves, she smiles. That bright red smile of hers glows almost as bright as the sun, making me melt in the front row.

"I'm glad you're all in the right place. I'll be your teacher for the semester, Roxie Hart."

Say what?

It takes everything in me to keep my jaw from gaping open at her revelation. How is *she* our teacher? She looks to be all of twenty-four if that.

It doesn't matter her age, though, because one thing I know for certain is that by the end of the semester, those red lips of hers will have touched every inch of my body.

Her being my teacher is only a temporary setback.

2

I'M BARELY LISTENING TO A WORD MY TEACHER IS SAYING because I'm trying to devise a plan that will get her under me when she tapes a piece of paper onto the whiteboard.

"Unfortunately, this semester, I don't have a teacher's assistant, nor are there any tutors for this particular class. Since I know some of you will need help on your research paper, I've opened up three slots where I will personally help three students. It's a first-come, first-serve basis, so if you think you're going to need help, please sign up today. I wish I could help more of you, but I don't have a lot of extra time on my hands. If none of the times I have work for you, we can meet and see if there's a better time that works for both of us, but I likely won't be able to do any other times."

Even though I don't need any help, I figure this is my way in to getting to spend some one-on-one time with my new teacher. While I feel bad I'll be taking away from someone who actually needs tutoring, I'm not going to change my mind. I can play dumb. At least for a while.

For the rest of the class, we go over the syllabus and the projects we'll have to do through the semester. When she dismisses class ten minutes early, I make a mad dash up to the front of the class to sign up. With my pen in hand, I sign up for Thursday nights at six, leaving the two other spots open.

With one last glance at Ms. Hart, who's got five students waiting to talk to her, I head out. I got what I wanted, and now I just have to figure out how I'm going to seduce my chemistry teacher. I know it's not going to be easy, but I think I'm up for the challenge.

With ten extra minutes to spare, I make my way to the library so I can grab a coffee at the Starbucks that resides inside. While I'm there, I decide to grab one for Walker as well.

Since I'm sure he's still in the music building, I beeline for the one room he's always in. Walker is exactly where I thought he would be—in front of a piano, scribbling on a piece of paper. The amount of talent this dude has in his pinky finger is more than most musicians have in their whole body.

I knock on the door, and when his head pops up, his dark hair falling over one eye, I hold up the other cup of coffee. Walker smiles and motions me inside.

"For me?" He questions even as he takes the offered coffee from my hands and takes a sip.

Sitting down on a chair a few feet away, I stretch my legs out and get comfortable. "I got out early and needed another fix."

"And you thought you'd bring me a cup?" He quirks an eyebrow at me.

"I didn't want to owe you," I quip.

He rolls his eyes and shakes his head. "You're a right asshole, you know that? I didn't do it so that you'd owe me. If anything, I'm the one who owes you. If it wasn't for your smart ass, I would have flunked out of college long ago."

I want to ask if it really matters when he's not going to finish up his degree anyway, but I bite my tongue.

Maybe Walker doesn't believe his band is going to be the next big thing, or maybe he just doesn't want to jinx it. Either way, I keep silent.

He stares at me for a moment before he looks back to the paper he was writing on when I knocked. "What's going on with you?"

"Who said there's anything going on with me?"

He doesn't look up as he says. "Because there's something different about you. Did some girl break your heart over the summer?"

I roll my eyes at him and shake my head. "There was no girl."

"But there is now?"

"No, not really." What am I supposed to say? That during the first class of my senior year, I decided I'm going to do everything in my power to fuck my teacher?

Turning his head slightly, he narrows his black eyes at me. "Don't lie to me, Merrick. We've known each other far too long for you to start now."

He's right. I can't remember a time when I've lied to him

since we met on the first day of kindergarten. He knows me better than anyone, even though we've grown apart as music has taken over his life and college mine.

Squaring my shoulders, I tell him. "I want to fuck my first-period teacher."

He barks out a laugh. "Well, that's new. I can't say I saw that one coming. So... what's stopping you?"

"Nothing, actually. I've already started laying the groundwork." I only hope Ms. Hart doesn't look into my grades and decides the spot would better off going to someone else.

"I don't see what the problem is then," he laughs.

Sinking back into the cool metal of the chair, I cross my ankle over my knee. "I never said there's a problem."

"No, I guess you didn't." He goes back to looking at what he was working on. It's then that I wonder if Walker has something on his mind.

Being the good friend that I am, I ask. "Is there something you want to get off your chest?"

"No," he shakes his head and lets his long hair flop in front of his face, which lets me know there is something.

We sit in silence for what has to be at least twenty minutes before he lets out a sigh and sets his pencil down. Still, I don't say a word. Whatever it is he wants to say isn't easy for him.

Shit.

Is he leaving sooner than I thought?

"You know the woman from Titan Records who's been coming to our practices and shows?"

Tall with long blondish-brown hair and alluring eyes with a

body made for sin. Yeah, I know who she is. Every guy who's been to one of Crimson Heat's shows knows.

"What about her?" I ask casually. I've seen the way my boy looks at her when he thinks no one is looking.

"You have to keep this between us. Not even the guys can know." His dark eyes drill into me, letting me know how serious he is.

"You know me. I won't say a word." Those assholes don't have my loyalty like he does. I'd keep any secret he tells me from them—from anyone. I'd bury a body for him.

"You didn't kill her, did you? I'm not really in the mood to bury a body today." Or ever.

"Fuck, dude, you're morbid in the morning," he smirks.

Maybe, but what the hell is he keeping a secret?

"We hooked up this past weekend."

That's all he says and then stares at me. For what, I don't know.

"Congratulations," I finally say after what seems like forever. I thought there would be more.

"No, you dumbass," he throws his hands in the air. "Not congratu-fucking-lations."

"Then what then?" I ask, exasperated. "Did she suck in bed?"

He growls, and there's murder in his eyes as he grits out, "Don't ever talk about her like that."

His teeth grind together as he glares at me until I finally relent and hold my hands up.

I didn't say anything about her. It was a mere question.

Then it hits me. Walker, my best friend since kindergarten, is in love. The only question is does he know it yet.

"I won't. There's no reason to just about go nuclear." When his jaw finally relaxes, I ask. "What's the problem then?" Because there's something that's eating him from the inside.

His fingers start to tap on the keys of the piano, but it makes no sound.

"She said it was a lapse in judgment and a one-time thing." Ouch.

"So, you're just going to give up?" That doesn't sound like him.

"Fuck, no," he laughs bitterly.

"Then I'm not seeing what the problem is," I state. He's never been one to back down from a challenge.

"She's into me. I know she is, but the problem is she can't date one of her clients. That's why she's freaking out."

That makes me think about what I want to do to dear Ms. Hart and how there's probably some rule stating she can't have sex with her students. Well, not just her per se, although it would be wise since she's hot as fuck, but all the teachers. I'm not saying there shouldn't be because there are plenty of girls here who could be taken advantage of— exactly the same way I want to take advantage of my chem teacher.

"Why don't you give her time? Show her you can be discreet, and maybe if she's interested in you, she'll hook up with you again." I throw that last part in to get a rise out of him, and it works.

He stands and is in front of me quicker than I thought he'd be. Looming over me, he shoves my shoulder and then barks out a laugh. "You're an asshole, you know that? Like she's not interested in me," he mumbles. I'm not sure if it's to himself or if he meant for me to hear him.

Walker's never had to *try* for a girl. They've always thrown themselves at him, and now that he's finally met his match, I can't wait to see what happens.

He gives my shoulder one last shove and then goes back to his seat in front of the piano like nothing happened. "So, what are you going to do about your teacher?"

I shake my head because I have no idea. I'll have to play it by ear and see how she responds to me when we're alone.

"Did you ever think we'd be where we are now talking about girls?" I laugh at the thought.

"The thing is, we're not talking about girls. We're talking about women. Women who know what they're doing and who don't play games." I'm not sure why he says the last part. I don't think it matters the age girls or women are; they can all play games. Hopefully, for us, we found the ones who don't.

3

"Mr. Landry, can I see you for a moment?" Ms. Hart calls after dismissing the class. It's been one week of class, and I'm supposed to meet with her tomorrow night.

Fuck.

I know she's going to call me out on not needing her help with my paper, and then I'm going to have to come up with a new plan.

Slipping my laptop in my backpack, I shove my phone in my back pocket and make my way over to her. She's sitting behind her desk with her sexy as fuck red glasses on.

Red is my new favorite color.

"Yes, Ms. Hart?" I stand and cross my arms over my chest and watch with satisfaction as she watches my muscles bulge with the movement.

She taps her pen on what looks to be her planner and bites her bottom lip. "I wanted to confirm you still want Thursday nights at six for help with your paper."

Standing up straighter, I question. "Why wouldn't I want it?"

"The others who signed up... well, they canceled. I don't have time for students who want to waste my time."

"I definitely won't waste your time and promise to be there right on time." Although I might have to kick the asses of the two others who canceled on her. What the fuck? "Surely there are others who would take their spots. I saw a decent-sized line waiting to sign up the other day."

"Yes, I asked, and they declined. It's strange." She watches the last of the class leave the room and then looks at me. "I'm surprised half the class didn't drop already."

Clasping my hands behind my back, I chuckle at her words. "If they're like me and plan to graduate this spring, they don't have that luxury. We need this class."

"Then why did they cancel?" She muses to herself.

"Maybe you intimidate them," I shrug because I have no idea. It pisses me off they've made her feel this way.

She narrows her eyes at me, but there's a little upturn of her lips as she says, "You better not cancel on me, or I'm going to think I've got bad breath or body odor. And I might just fail you."

"Trust me, you don't have either. In fact, you smell..." I take in her scent, but I can't place it at first. It eludes me until it pops into my head. "You smell like vanilla and honey."

"Really?" She pulls a strand of hair in front of her nose and sniffs.

"Yeah. Why is that?" Does she use some other fragrance?

"I've just never had anyone say they can smell my shampoo and body wash. You must have a good nose."

I've never thought of myself as having a good sense of smell. In fact, normally, I can barely smell anything except for my roommates' sweaty gym clothes.

I shrug it off.

"When we meet tomorrow night, please have some research paper topics picked out. I can help you choose one, and we can start going over the finer points of what you want to talk about." She sets her pen down and then looks up at me. "I do understand this paper is a big part of your grade and required for you to graduate. I hope I can be of help."

"I have no doubt you'll help me." I fight back the smirk that tries desperately to take over my face.

She picks up a stack of papers and starts to go through them. "I'm sorry to keep you so long. You should go before you're late to your next class."

I don't mention I don't have another class for another three hours. If I can help it, I don't take any classes before ten in the morning. Unfortunately for me, her class is at eight, three days a week. At least I have an incentive to get up in the morning. If she was some ugly old bastard, I'd probably sleep right through my alarm.

I give her a little wave as students start to file inside the classroom. I guess her schedule is packed, and that's why she has an eight am class. Either that or she's a morning person. "I'll see you tomorrow at six."

"Yes, I'll see you tomorrow, Mr. Landry."

There's something about the way she calls me mister that

has my blood pumping in all the wrong places right now. I haven't gotten hard in a classroom since middle school, when my English teacher used to wear low-cut blouses and bend over to read off her desk, giving all the boys a show. I swear she knew what she was doing. If we ever stepped out of line, she'd go to her desk to start to write us up, and then we'd get a peek at her perky breasts and stop whatever we were doing to drool. Needless to say, we tried to get in trouble all the time.

Instead of going to see how Walker's doing, I decide to head back to the house I share with two other guys and get some more sleep. My house isn't much. In fact, it's a fucking dump, but it's what we can afford, and it's so much cheaper than living in the dorms. My poor mom was working double shifts to be able to afford to pay for my food and lodging. That's when I found a cheap house to rent through the school year and found two roommates to share the expenses with.

It's about a five-minute walk to get to the house from campus. The day is starting to warm up, and I know when I have to go to my classes later, I'm going to be sweating my balls off.

The house is quiet when I walk inside. Not that I expected anything different. Neither of my roommates has class until eleven, so they're likely sound asleep—like I should be.

Leaving my backpack by the front door, I step out of my shoes and head straight for my room. I hit the switch to turn on the ceiling fan and throw myself face-first on the bed.

I try to fall asleep, but I can't get my fucking chemistry teacher out of my head. The way she wears tight skirts that mold to her perfect ass and those sexy red lips of hers.

I give up the fight and open my nightstand, where I pull out a bottle of lotion and a box of tissues.

Slipping my shorts down, I pull out my semi-hard cock. I pump a good amount of lotion onto my hand and start to stroke. If nothing else, the skin of my cock is going to be the softest in all of Willow Bay with how many times I jerk thinking about my teacher.

I've found the only way to get her out of my head is to get myself off to thoughts of her. Since I first laid eyes on her I've already jerked myself off eight times in the last week.

Only after I've imagined taking Ms. Hart with her bent over her desk and smacking her ass until it's as good and red as her lipstick do I fall asleep.

4

I wonder if Ms. Hart will notice that I showered, put on my best casual clothes, and put on a little aftershave for our date, I mean tutoring session tonight?

It would feel more like a date if we were meeting somewhere else besides her office, although I do like the thought of it just being the two of us alone together. Since it is dinner time, I stop by the only pizza place in town and grab something for us to eat.

Arriving a few minutes early, I find the door to her office is closed, and I'm not sure what to do. Do I wait? Or knock on the door? I hear voices, but I can't make out what they're saying. Whoever's in there, I'm only giving them five minutes because, after that, they'll be interfering with my time with her.

Sitting down on the lone chair in the hall, I place the pizza box on my lap and pull out my phone to see where Walker's playing this weekend. There's no doubt that he'll be playing somewhere, and I only hope it's close. My old car gets the worst gas mileage, and a trip down to LA would seriously cut into my savings.

Merrick: Hey, are you playing this weekend?

Walker: Are you coming?

I roll my eyes because it's like he knows if he gets me to say yes, I'll drive the three fucking hours to LA or wherever he's playing to keep my word.

Merrick: Depends on where. I can't spend my whole night driving. I've already got a shit ton of homework.

Walker: Do you think you can drive the twenty minutes it will take you to go to the next town over?

Merrick: Yes, fucker.
Of course, I can.
Send me the deets and I'll be there.

Walker: Cool. I'll see you Saturday.

I LOOK AT THE TIME AND SEE THERE'S ONE MINUTE LEFT before it turns six o'clock. It's probably in my best interest not to be a total asshole the first time we're going to spend time alone, but it's looking like the asshole in me is going to take over and ruin my plan. I can barely sit still.

Annoyed, I stand, about ready to barge inside when the door opens, and some guy is standing there hugging my woman. I want to rage and beat my chest with my fists, but I hold back. Barely.

He barely glances at me, limping as he passes. Limp aside, he's a tall, athletic fucker who I've never seen before.

Ms. Hart moves to peek out her door. "Mr. Landry, I'm glad you didn't cancel on me. I thought it was something I did in class to scare all the kids away."

I'm not sure what she could be talking about. She's done nothing that would scare anyone away. In fact, all she's done is make me obsessed with her. Okay, so maybe that doesn't make me very objective.

"I wish I could tell you why, but I have no clue." I think of my class, and while I've had a few classes with most of them, I don't talk to them unless we have to do a project together. "I don't really know any of them all that well to get the four-one-one on why they're running scared from you."

We both laugh at my statement because who the hell would run from her. No one. Instead, she might be the one running from me once she figures out what I have planned for her.

Moving out of the doorway, she goes to sit behind her desk. Fuck, how am I going to put any moves on her with the desk in between us? "Why don't we get started, shall we?"

Sitting down in the chair across from her, I hold up the pizza box. "I wasn't sure if you'd be hungry, so I got us a pizza."

She picks up her pen and then sits it back down again. "That's very sweet of you, Mr. Landry."

"You can call me Merrick. Mr. Landry sounds so… formal," I laugh. I don't want this to feel like a business meeting.

"Okay, Merrick," she says my name like she's tasting it on her tongue and likes it. "You can call me Roxie, but only when we're not in class. I don't want the other students to be calling me by my first name."

"I can do that." Internally I'm fist-pumping because I'm already getting to know her, and she's letting her guard down. "I wasn't sure what you'd like, so I got a half veggie, half meat lovers."

"Oh, you really didn't have to do that, but I do appreciate it. While I don't normally skip lunch, a student needed some help today and ate up all my time. Next time, I'll bring the food. How does that sound?"

Sounds like a date.

I don't say that, though. Instead, I agree and try to figure out how we can meet somewhere else for our next session.

I hold the pizza box out to her, and she takes a slice. I take one as well and start eating because I'm fucking starving. I missed lunch before my classes because I was too busy thinking of her to do anything else.

She takes a delicate bite while I'm shoving half the slice in my mouth. "I know it's early, but have you decided on the topic for your research paper?"

Fuck, she's getting straight to the point.

"Not yet. I've picked a few and thought I'd run them by you and see what you think." The economic side of chemistry really isn't my thing, so I don't know what I want to write a ten-page paper on. If I had a choice, it would either be nothing or her, but neither are my choices.

We talk through a few of the ideas I have for my research, and then she sits back in her seat and brings her pen to her mouth.

I've never wanted to be an inanimate object more in my life than I want to be that damn pen. She's always messing with it, and at first, I didn't think anything of it. Just that it's a normal pen, but as I can't take my eyes away from where she's got it between those red lips of hers, I see that it's not a regular pen. It's expensive and a glossy red to match those damn lips of hers.

"Did you bring your laptop with you?" She finally asks.

Now it's time for me to decide if I'm going to tell her the truth or if I'm going to lie so I can hopefully get around to the other side of the desk.

As much as I hate lying, I do anyway. "I left it at home. The battery was almost dead, and I wasn't sure if you'd have a place in here for me to plug into. I'll make sure to bring it with me next time." The lie feels heavy on my tongue, but when she rolls her chair to the right to make space for me, my guilt disappears.

"Next time, bring it, but for now, come around here so you can see what I'm seeing. After hearing your ideas, I think you can do more. The only problem is, I don't know how much information is on the internet you can use for your paper. We might have to spend a couple of our sessions in the library." She bites down on her bottom lip, and it's all I can do to not remove it with my thumb and ask her to bite me instead.

She clicks around on the screen and starts going to different websites, but I don't pay any attention. Being this close to her and her vanilla and honey scent is driving me wild. It's all I can do to keep my hands and body to myself. I want to pounce on top of her like a lion and make her mine.

Shaking my head, I try to follow along, but I fail spectacularly. All the blood has traveled from my brain to my dick, where it's currently throbbing behind my zipper, causing me pain. If there was any way to adjust myself without drawing attention to the bulge in my jeans, I would, but there's no way in hell she won't notice.

Although maybe it would be a good thing. Maybe this is what I need to get her to start thinking of me as someone other than her student.

Still, it's too early. The first time we're alone together, I don't want her to think I'm some creeper and cancel the rest of our sessions. So instead, I shift in my seat, making it look like I'm trying to get a better look at what she's showing me.

But it's no use. Unless I physically move my dick from behind my zipper, I'm going to be in pain.

The words she's saying barely register. Why does she have such a profound effect on me? I've never been this hard over a girl, or so... obsessed is the best word to describe it. She's constantly on my mind, in my dreams, in my fantasies, and being this close to her is only going to make it harder for me to forget about her until class tomorrow morning.

"I can tell I've given you a lot to think about. Why don't you use the week to decide on what you want to research, and then I'll help you get started next Thursday. How does that sound?"

"Sounds good." I clear my throat of the lust that's built up inside while I've sat beside her and stand. I turn and adjust myself before I look back at her. "Do you want to meet in the library next time? I can reserve a room if you want."

Ms. Hart leans back in her chair and looks me over. Like really looks me over like this is the first time she's seeing me, and I can't help but stand a little taller.

Her mouth parts and her dark brown eyes sweep up and down my body. Maybe this won't be so hard after all.

She shakes her head and looks to her computer screen for a moment. "Why don't we meet here again next week, and we'll go from there. If you decide on a topic before we meet, you can email me, and I'll see what resources the library has."

And just when I thought she'd be easy to get naked. That's okay, though. The first time I take her, I want it to be here in her office. I want to shove all the papers off her desk as I stare down at her sweet ass bent over her desk.

I just need to step up my game.

5

———

Standing by the bar as I wait for Crimson Heat to come on, I swear I spot my chemistry teacher in the crowd. I blink a few times as if it's the lighting playing tricks on me. If it's anything, it's my mind playing tricks. I've never had a woman under my skin like this, and nothing's even happened between us.

Yet.

When the woman across the room still looks like my new obsession, I shake my head and rub my eyes. It can't be her. Why would she be at a bar in Loganville?

If it is her, I need to be closer, and if it's not, maybe I can pretend she is Roxie and use her to get my teacher out of my system.

I signal the bartender for two more beers, not wanting to come to her empty-handed. I slide him a ten-dollar bill when he sets them down in front of me.

I look down at my wrinkled shirt and stained jeans. Why

didn't I do laundry this week so I'd have something to wear? If it is Roxie, she's going to see what a slob I normally am. I groan but continue walking toward her. Tonight could be my chance. We're away from school, and there's alcohol involved—at least on my part.

With only about a foot of space separating us, I stop and take her in. From here, I can almost smell her vanilla and honey scent. She's swaying to the beat of the music playing over the speakers until Walker's band comes on. She's got the front of her hair pinned up, showing the delicate column of her neck and her pale skin. I'm driven by the need to mark her.

Almost as if she can feel my eyes on her, Roxie turns and looks startled to see me for a second, but then the corners of her lips lift. Eliminating the distance between us, I tip one of the beers toward her and clank it against her plastic cup.

Leaning in close, I speak loud enough for her to hear me. "I thought that was you. Do you want a beer?"

Her nose scrunches up as she looks down at her full drink. "I'm not really a beer girl, but I'm not sure it can be worse than this." She tilts her cup in my direction, and it looks like fruit punch. Leaning down to smell it, I nearly swat it out of her hand because it smells like gasoline.

"I'm pretty sure there's not much that smells worse than that. Have you drunk any?"

"Not yet. I've been working up my courage to take a sip. I guess you can say you saved me from poisoning myself with this…" she shakes the cup. "Whatever this is."

"What did you order?" I trade her the beer I got for her with the offending drink.

"I'm not sure. They don't have many options here, so I said to give me the special."

"Yeah, this is more of a beer joint. I'm a guy, and even I try not to use the bathroom here."

She moves closer as she takes a sip of beer. "I'm taking it you've been here before."

I nod and get closer still until there's barely any room separating us. "A few times. My best friend is in the band." She looks around, taking in the cramped, dark room. "I take it this is your first time here," she nods and continues to sway to the beat. "So, what made you decide to come out tonight?"

She turns away, and I don't miss the blush staining her cheeks even in the dark lighting. Taking a large sip of her beer, which makes her face scrunch up, she finally turns back to me. "This is embarrassing. I was supposed to meet a date, but he backed out at the last minute."

I growl at the thought of her on a date with anyone else. Her brows furrow for a moment but then quickly even out.

"Are you here alone?" She asks, sounding curious.

I shrug because I guess you could call it that. "I came alone, but once the show's over, I'll hang out with the guys. Until then, we can hang out if you want."

"Ugh," she sighs and takes another swig of her beer. "I feel like a loser. First, my date cancels on me, and now you're taking pity on me."

I bump her elbow with mine. "It's not a hardship hanging out with you. In fact, I think you're a cool chick."

She lays her hand on my arm while smiling up at me. "You're just saying that to make me feel better, but thank you."

All I can think about is her touch. The way her petite hand feels so soft against my skin as little zaps of electricity shoot straight to my cock.

When she removes her hand, I can finally think straight. "I'm not that nice of a guy," I admit.

"You're being nice tonight."

Because I have an ulterior motive, but she doesn't need to know that.

The music cuts off, and the lights dim even more, indicating Crimson Heat is about to come out on stage.

Kenton is the first one out, going to sit behind his drum kit. Cross and Greer are next out, picking up their guitars and plugging them in. They strum a few cords and make some adjustments. The second Walker steps out on stage and walks to the microphone, the crowd goes wild. Even though they're only playing in a bar, it certainly doesn't feel like it in this moment. It sounds like a sold-out stadium.

Roxie claps and screams right along with the rest of the crowd with a huge grin on her face.

"Hello, Loganville," Walker shouts into the microphone. "How are you this fine Saturday night?"

If the noise the crowd is making is anything to go by, they're having the best Saturday of their lives.

Roxie can't stop whistling and staring up at Walker in awe. I can't believe she's into that broody motherfucker. She turns to me with bright eyes full of excitement.

"Which one is your friend?"

Turning back, I look up to Walker, who's getting the crowd

riled up. "The singer." I lift my chin to Walker, and he points directly at me.

"Do you see that beautiful bastard right there?" Walker keeps pointing at me with an evil smile on his face.

What the fuck is he doing? I swear if he fucks this up for me, I'm going to kill him. He'll never have the chance to become famous.

The entire room looks at me, and for the first time in my life, I want to duck and run away.

"That man, Merrick, is my best friend. He has been since we met on the first day of kindergarten. He's been by my side encouraging me to follow my dreams of being up on stage since we met. If it wasn't for him, I would have been thrown out of Willow Bay at least a dozen times. Thank you, man, for always believing in me."of being up on stage since we met. If it wasn't for him, I would have been thrown out of Willow Bay at least a dozen times. Thank you, man, for always believing in me."

I lift my beer to salute him.

"Give them what they came for," I yell.

Kenton counts down by hitting his sticks together, and then they start playing. The whole crowd sings along and dances in a tantalizing rhythm.

Watching Roxie experience Crimson Heat for the first time is exhilarating. Seeing someone fall in love with their music is unlike anything I've ever experienced. I can't imagine how Walker and the rest of them feel every time they play.

Once the first round of songs ends, I turn to Roxie, who, along with everyone else, seems to be having the time of her life. "Have you ever heard their music before?"

"No, but now I want more. Can I download their music or buy a CD or something?" She bounces as the next song starts.

"Nothing yet, but they're working on it. I'll be shocked if they aren't signed on to Titan Records by Christmas."

"Really, so soon?"

I'm sure it doesn't feel soon to Walker, who's been working on having his music in people's hands for the last six years.

Draining the last of my beer, I hold it up. "Do you want another?"

She pulls out her phone and looks at the time. "Sure, why not?"

"I'll be back in a few minutes with new drinks."

I don't take my eyes off Roxie as I make my way to the bar, not caring who I bump into. It only takes a few minutes for me to grab two more beers, but by the time I'm making my way back to her, there's some fucker trying to get her to dance with him.

I've heard of people who say they see red when they're angry, but I never believed it. That is until I see this motherfucker, who's got no right to put his hands on Roxie, palm the curves of her hips. Pulling her against him, he grinds into her ass. When I see her try to pry his hands off and he pulls her tighter to him, I lose it. Now, I'm not one normally prone to anger, but my world goes completely red as I charge over to them and push him off her.

He shoves me back a step and gets in my face. "What the hell, dude? What's your problem?"

Not backing down, I stand to my full height and use the

three inches I have over him. "The lady doesn't want your hands on her."

"Merrick," Roxie calls from beside me as she tries to get in between us. "It's okay. Please, let's just go."

"Listen to your girlfriend," he taunts.

Out of the corner of my eye, I see Walker motion toward us, and I instantly feel like shit that I could very well be ruining his show. It doesn't make me back down, though. This asshole needs to learn that you can't touch a woman without her permission.

"Back away, Roxie. This guy needs to be taught a lesson," I narrow my eyes at him.

The smirk he gives me pushes me over the edge, and I'm seconds away from punching him in the face when I see security making its way to us. That must have been what Walker was doing—calling them to break up the fight.

Whoever this asshole is, he must see them too. For one brief moment, I think he's going to run, but instead, he rears back and punches me straight in the nose. Pain explodes in my face making me see stars for a few seconds, and when it clears, he's already being hauled out of the venue. Too bad they didn't come a few seconds later, so I could have gotten my hit in.

"Oh my god, Merrick, you're bleeding. Let's get you to the bathroom and get you cleaned up." Roxie grabs my hand and is pulling me in the direction of the restrooms before I have a chance to tell her I'm alright.

A little blood never hurt anyone.

Every few seconds, she glances back at me with a worried look as she tries to push people out of the way.

It's then that I notice the band is back to playing. I look up to where Walker is and see his eyes tracking my every move as he continues to sing into the microphone. I wave at him, letting him know I'm fine. I'm better than fine. I've got Roxie holding my hand and rushing me away from the hundred or so people who don't give a damn about us.

People aren't moving out of our way fast enough, going by the annoyed but determined look on her face, so I take matters into my own hands. Picking up my pace, I push ahead of Roxie and use my shoulder on anyone who doesn't get out of our way. A few people look annoyed until they look at me and then step out of the way.

I don't know if it's because they realize I'm friends with Walker or if it's that I look that bad. I can feel liquid trailing down my chin. Reaching up to wipe it away, I come away with red all over my hand. I look down to see if any has made it onto my shirt, but it's dark, and so is the room, making it difficult to see much of anything.

Once in the hallway, where it's a little quieter, we come face to face with a long ass line to the women's restroom. Coming around in front of me, Roxie frowns as she takes me in. She looks to the line and then to the non-existent one for the men's restroom.

"Come on," she pushes open the door but takes a step back at the dirty restroom. "Is it always like this?"

"Here? Yeah, that's why I said I try not to use it," I chuckle.

"At least you don't have any open wounds. If you did, you'd probably get an infection."

She isn't wrong. This bathroom is what horror movies are

made of. There's not a clean spot anywhere you look, and there's used paper towels and toilet paper littering the floor along with puddles of brown liquid. The sink has brown smudges all over it —and let's not even get started with the smell.

"Let's hurry this up. It's taking everything in me to not throw up," she says before holding her breath.

"I'm fine," I try to assure her.

"No, you're not. We need to clean up the blood and try to get your nose to stop bleeding." She starts to rummage through her purse, looking for I don't know what.

Opening the door, I start to push her out. "I'll get some clean paper towels and wet them. You can wait out in the hall."

I don't want to be in the bathroom any longer than necessary, and we can do whatever she wants out in the hall. I'm probably going to need to boil my hands after touching the sink and paper dispenser.

A minute later, I come out of the bathroom with a stack of soaking wet paper towels to a relieved-looking Roxie.

Before I can say a word, she grabs the stack and starts wiping my face, starting with my chin. "I can't believe that asshole hit you," she shakes her head and huffs. It's cute she's angry trying to protect my honor when it was me who was trying to protect hers.

"I can't either, especially when security was coming. Hopefully, he won't be allowed back in the place," I grumble.

"Your friend needs to find better places to play because this," she points over my shoulder to the bathroom door. "Is the most disgusting place I've ever encountered. Are all men's restrooms like that?"

"Not that bad, but they can be pretty… gross. Most of the time, they're clean. Don't let that one ruin your experiences in men's bathrooms."

She grimaces and shakes her head. "I don't plan to spend much time in one ever again if I can help it. I might have PTSD and never be able to use a public restroom again after seeing that."

I want to say it wasn't that bad, but yeah, it was. The smell alone would do the trick. I swear it's a close replica of the bathroom in that Saw movie.

"Now, stop moving so I can get you cleaned up," she rests one hand on my cheek and uses the other to wipe the now-drying blood away. "At least it looks like your nose stopped bleeding." She stops what she's doing and looks up at me. She's shorter without her heels on tonight, making her have to crane her neck to meet my gaze. "Thank you for coming to the rescue." She bites on her lower lip, and my dick goes from a semi ready to thrust inside of her in a nanosecond. "I… I started to get scared until you arrived."

And there went my dick.

I hate that she was scared.

"He shouldn't have put his hands on you," I spit out.

"I know," she says softly. It does little to tame the beast inside that wants to go find that guy and rip his head off.

Her thumb caresses my cheek, and it takes everything in me not to kiss her right here and now. I'm not sure why I'm holding back when I want nothing more, but I do.

One touch to the side of my nose and the pain that feels

like someone's jabbing a metal rod up my nose and straight to my brain has me pulling back.

"I'm sorry. Shit," she moves back into my space, and this time lightly dabs around my nose. She does this a few times before she takes a step back and looks as if she's trying to observe her handy work.

"I think I got it all." She looks pained as she takes me in. "You're probably going to have a black eye tomorrow. Maybe two."

"Not really my best look, but I'll live."

She looks down the hall and then back to me as she worries her bottom lip. "Do you get in many fights?"

"Can't say that I do. I'm a pretty chill guy, or at least I like to think I am. I've had a couple of altercations, but nothing major. That asshole…" I don't want to think about him. If I do, I'll want to hunt him down, and then I'll probably get kicked out of school for what I'd do to him.

Taking me by the arm, Roxie turns us, so we're facing each other, but others can get by in the hall. "Hey, don't let him ruin your night." Her voice is soft and seductive, and the way she's looking at me, I can't fight what I'm feeling any longer.

Sweeping down, I envelop her face in my hands and crush my mouth to hers. For a brief second, she stiffens and then opens for me. My tongue sweeps in, and all I taste is heaven. Besides the beer from earlier, I can also taste something that is distinctly Roxie—and I like it.

Angling her head for better access, I plunder her waiting mouth and grind my dick against her stomach.

Roxie gasps. Putting her hands to my chest, she pushes, and I immediately step back, giving her space.

"Merrick," she says my name in a breathy whisper. "We can't. It's wrong. I'm your teacher."

"I know exactly who you are, but I don't care. I've wanted to kiss you—and more—from the second I saw you standing in front of my class. I won't deny I was a little disappointed when I found out you were the teacher and not the TA."

"Because you know it's wrong," she moves to step back, but I grip her waist and pull her to me.

"There's nothing wrong with the way you make me feel. In fact, everything about it is right."

"No, it's not. It's wrong, and I could get fired." She pushes away again, and this time I let her go. She needs her space, but I know she feels some type of connection to me. Otherwise, she wouldn't have kissed me back.

With my dick screaming in my pants not to let her go, I watch as Roxie hastily walks down the hallway. When she reaches the opening, she turns back. I expect to see regret in her eyes, but all I see is lust.

6

    ——————

For the entire week, Roxie has been ignoring me. When I try to talk to her after class, she gives me a weak excuse as to why she has to go and then leaves like the room is on fire.

I'm surprised she hasn't canceled our tutoring session tonight. I'm not sure why I call it that. I guess it's technically called tutoring, but all she's really doing is helping me find resources and guide me on my research paper. At least she doesn't seem like she'll give us lots of homework, which is good because my other classes are burying me.

When I get to Roxie's office, I find another student from my class waiting outside in the only chair. What the fuck is she doing here? I take the space on the other side of the hall and lean against the wall as I stare at Roxie's closed door.

Did she forget about our session?

No, I don't believe that for a second.

Right as my phone indicates it's six o'clock on the dot, her door swings open, and there she is with a serene smile on her ruby red lips. She looks to me and then quickly to the girl sitting in the chair. I've had a few classes with her, but I have no idea what her name is.

"Casey, Merrick, come in. I hope you don't mind, but I can only meet for thirty minutes tonight. I have an appointment at seven that I need to get to."

"Oh, that's fine," Casey says, moving into the room, her long brown hair sliding over her face like usual. She's always hiding.

"Is it for a date?" I ask as I walk by her.

"That's none of your business since I'm the teacher, and you're the student."

Oh, she has no idea how much it is my business. And I will find out. I'll follow her to wherever she's going, and I'll ruin her damn date if I have to. There's no way in hell I'm going to let her get involved with some other man.

Roxie narrows her eyes at me as if she can tell what I'm thinking. Tough shit. I guess she should have answered my question when she had the chance.

I sit back in the seat across from Ms. Hart's desk with my laptop out the entire time while she and Casey talk about Casey's research topic. I'm not doing any research. All I can do is look at her while I pretend to be doing something other than planning how I'm going to sabotage her date.

"I'm sorry to cut this short, but I really must go. Casey, if you need any more help, I think we're going to meet next week at the library to find more research materials. You're more than welcome to join us."

I want to protest, but instead, I train my glare on Casey and watch as she shrinks into her chair beside Roxie and stutters out. "I think I'll be good, but thank you."

I'm such an asshole. Casey's never done anything to me, and now I've gone and scared her. I'm not that guy. I can't let this crazy obsession I have with my chemistry teacher turn me into a raving lunatic.

I let a small smile break through and offer an olive branch. "If you need help, please join us."

"Um… that's okay. I normally work on Thursday nights, anyway. I just wanted to make sure I was on the right track. Thank you for helping me, Ms. Hart."

"You're most welcome, Casey. I'm here anytime you need help," Roxie stands and starts to pack up. I wait until Casey's gone to close the door and see if I can get some answers.

I press up against her back but keep my hands to myself because I know once I touch her, I won't be able to stop. "Are you really that scared of me that you had to have little Casey act as a buffer?

She stiffens and doesn't bother to turn and look at me. "I'm not scared of anything, least of all you, Mr. Landry. Now, if you don't mind, I would appreciate it if you'd back off. I really do have to go."

I don't budge from my spot. "Are you going on a date?"

"Again, it's none of your business, but no, I'm not going on a date. I have a doctor's appointment to go to."

"Are you okay?" I ask instantly.

I'm pissed she had Casey cockblock our time together, but I don't want anything bad to happen to her.

"I'm fine. It's not for me," she pushes my chest and steps

around me to head down the hall. "If you would please go now, I need to leave. I'll see you tomorrow morning in class."

I'm not buying that the doctor's appointment isn't for her. Why would she be going then? No, I think she's going on a date, and I'm determined to cockblock her the same way she used Casey.

Stepping outside, I realize, like most days, I walked to school today. Deciding I'm not going to let that hinder my stalking, I run from the science building all the way to my house. I know it won't take long for her to pack and lock up, so I run like my ass is on fire. Throwing my backpack in the passenger seat, I reverse out of my driveway and haul ass back to the science building's parking lot.

Once I'm in the parking lot that I think Roxie parks in, I realize I have no idea what car she drives. I guess my stalking skills are lacking. It's then I notice a red sports car coming from my left. It zips out in front of me and hits the street.

I'm betting that's her.

She certainly loves her red.

Since I've never actually followed anyone before but have seen it plenty of times in the movies and on TV, I try to keep my distance, so she doesn't realize she's got a crazy stalker on her tail.

If me crowding her in her office earlier didn't piss her off, finding me on her bumper definitely will. Turning on the radio, I blast Panic at the Disco as we make our way out of Willow Bay and head in the direction of Newton.

Why is she going to Newton?

Still, I keep at least three car lengths between us. About

thirty minutes later, we're taking the first exit into Newton. Now that we're back on city streets, I hang back a little further in case she's wondering why there's a dark car following her.

In a way, I hope she notices me. Otherwise, it's scary to think that some random person could be tailing her, and she'd never know.

It's not long until we're pulling up to a medical building. I park in the back and slowly walk up to where Roxie parks her car, giving her enough time to get out. I know I should probably get back in my car and head home, but for some inexplicable reason, I can't.

When I see the man who came out of her office last week get out of the passenger side, I almost lose it.

Who the fuck is this guy?

Roxie turns abruptly and looks back at me. "Merrick, what are you doing here?"

Shit, I must have made some sort of noise.

The man with her turns and looks at me with annoyance clearly written on his face.

He takes a menacing step toward me before he looks back at her.

"Who is this asshole?" We both ask at the same time.

He whirls back and glares at me.

Roxie looks up to the sky for a brief moment and murmurs something before she looks back and forth between us.

"Declan, this is my student, Merrick." She narrows her eyes when she turns to me. "Merrick, this is my brother, Declan. I don't know why you're here, but we don't have time for this. We need to get inside for a doctor's appointment. Now, if you don't mind, I'll see you tomorrow *in class.*"

Why do I feel like if she could, Ms. Hart would send me to the principal's office?

Maybe following her wasn't the best idea.

7

I COULDN'T SLEEP LAST NIGHT. ONCE I GOT HOME, I realized how wrong it was of me to follow Roxie. Not only from school, but to another town where she was taking her brother to see a doctor. I don't know his story, but the tight facial features and his limp let me know the guy's in a lot of pain—pain he's probably trying to hide from his sister. I have a feeling she doesn't know the true depth of what he's hiding.

Since I haven't slept, I get out of bed and force myself to get ready. I arrive thirty minutes before class starts, hoping that if I'm standing outside the classroom when Roxie unlocks the door, she'll let me talk to her and apologize.

Time is ticking down until class, and now that I'm out in the world, I'm tired, and all I want to do is crawl back in my bed and sleep. Ten minutes before class is set to begin, I see Roxie come around the corner. When she spots me, she halts in her tracks for a split second and then continues like it's any other day.

"Ms. Hart," I barely get her name out before her chestnut eyes narrow at me, and I see the firm set of her mouth. "I'm sorry about last night. I don't know what I was thinking."

"You're damn right. You didn't know what you were thinking because you weren't. I told you I was going to a doctor's appointment that wasn't mine. Why you felt the need to follow me there, I'll never know."

"I thought you were making it up. That maybe you had a date," I try to explain feebly.

"And what difference would have made if I was on a date? What would you have done, Mr. Landry? My dating life is none of your concern," she hisses as she unlocks the door.

"I'm sorry. I really am." I want to tell her if I could stop the pull I feel toward her, I would, but if I said those words, she would make sure she's never alone with me again. "I promise it won't happen again."

She rounds on me with fire in her eyes. "You're damn right it won't happen again because if it does, I will go to the Dean and tell him how you stalked me and sexually harassed me."

"I'll admit I shouldn't have followed you, but I've never sexually—"

"What do you call what happened at the bar?" Her hands go to her lush hips, and it's then I take in her attire. I swear she's trying to kill me with her tight as sin skirts that conform to every sexy curve she has from her waist to her knees. "Hmm?"

Fuck, did she say something? "What?" I ask, meeting her eyes.

"I asked what you were doing right that instant. You were looking at me like I'm a piece of meat."

"Trust me when I say that meat was the last thing I was thinking about."

"Mr. Landry, you're two seconds away from being kicked out of my classroom, and we both know what that will mean."

It means I won't graduate this year.

Fuck.

"I'm sorry, Ms. Hart. You bring out a side of me that I'm not used to. I can't control myself," I admit.

She opens her mouth to say something, but a couple of girls walk into class, interrupting her.

"We'll finish this later. Meet me in my office tonight at six o'clock. If you try anything or are late, you can forget about ever coming back to class."

Her threat shocks me. Would she really fuck over my life that easily? Going by the hard glint in her eyes, I have no doubt I'm hanging on by a thread.

I nod and take my seat. I can't concentrate on the class or what she's saying when normally I'm hanging on her every word. Instead, all I can think about is how I'm going to make this better. How can I make her see me the way I see her?

8

———

I'M SITTING OUTSIDE MS. HART'S OFFICE AT FIVE-THIRTY to make sure I'm not late. I didn't go back home and sleep after class like I wanted to. No, all I could do is wonder how I was going to fix the monumental fuck up I'd created.

I'll be surprised if she doesn't cancel the rest of our sessions if not kick me out of class.

Roxie comes from the opposite end of the hall and doesn't even bother to look at me as she unlocks her door and sweeps inside. Nor does she bother to look back at me to see if I follow.

"Close the door behind you, Mr. Landry." Her voice is stern, unlike the usual soft tone she speaks with.

I look at her and then do as she says before I take a step toward her.

"Roxie," I start, but when I see the fire in her eyes, I begin again. "Ms. Hart, I want to apologize for last night. I should never have done what I did, and I understand if you feel like you can't tutor me any longer."

"Listen, my brother is a very private man, and he's been through a lot. I'm not condoning what you did by following me yesterday, but he doesn't deserve to have his space and privacy invaded like that."

"I completely agree. I let my imagination get away with me, and…" Fuck. How can I tell her I'm obsessed with her and that I couldn't help myself?

Some of the tension from her shoulders releases as she stands there and looks at me. "And you what?"

"It's going to sound crazy, and you'll probably want to get a restraining order against me once I tell you," I state, clasping my hands in front of me.

"Have you followed me other places? Is that why you were at the bar?"

"No, nothing like that. I told you I'm friends with Walker, and if it weren't for the band, there's no way in hell I would have been in that dump."

She nods as if she believes me. "Then what is it?"

"I've never felt this pull toward another human being before in my life—not even my high school or college girlfriends. I'm insanely attracted to you if you haven't already figured that out yet, and it makes me do and think crazy things."

She tilts her head to the side as her eyes spark with curiosity. "What kind of crazy things?"

"I've pictured fucking you all over this office and in the classroom," I stupidly and freely admit.

"Is that so?" She hums and licks her lips, making my dick jump in my pants.

"The simplest things you do get me hard for the entire day

until I have no other choice but to take matters into my own hands."

"Are you saying you don't have a girlfriend?" She moves around to sit on the corner of her desk. It makes her skirt hitch up her creamy thighs, and I want nothing more than to run my hands over her smooth skin and taste every inch of her.

"No girlfriend. We broke up at the beginning of our junior year." I try to adjust myself in a way that isn't obvious, but one flair of her eyes, and I know she knows the situation going on in my pants.

"A fuck buddy then?"

"No one but my own hand," I tell her truthfully.

Her gaze flits to the door and then back at me. "How old are you, Merrick?"

"Twenty-two," I blurt out. At least I didn't say, "I'm legal." Nothing could be more of a turnoff than that. "How old are you?"

My eyes follow those red lips of hers as she smirks in front of me. "Haven't you ever heard you should never ask a lady how old she is?"

"A time or two. But seriously, what's the big deal? I'm not sure how you got the job, but you look all of twenty-four, maybe twenty-five."

"Well, I'm a little bit older than that. And the big deal, as you say, is it's against school policy for a teacher to sleep with any of their students."

"It's a good thing I don't want to sleep with you, then. I just want to fuck your brains out."

"You knew what I meant, and if you didn't, you're not as

smart as I thought you were. Let me ask you something, Mr. Landry. Did you sign up for my help because you truly needed it or because you thought you might be able to charm your way into my skirt if you persisted enough?"

When she puts it like that, it sounds bad. Really bad. I know I should probably lie if I actually want to get my dick wet, but I can't. She asked, and now I'm going to tell her the truth.

"I didn't need help with writing my research paper, just with picking a topic. But I didn't think I could wear you down, and all of a sudden, you'd flip up your skirt for me."

She stands and moves around to sit behind her desk. She steeples her fingers and rests her chin on them. "At least you were honest."

"Are you going to stop our sessions?" I don't know why I ask when I just told her I don't need them. I guess it's because I want to hear her say our alone time is over.

"I didn't say that," she answers and then bites her lower lip.

A low growl reverberates through me at the sight. "You really have no idea the kind of temptress you are, do you?"

Her cheeks flush as she shakes her head. "You can't flatter yourself into a better grade."

Does she think I'm lying? I'm sitting here telling her that I'm constantly hard for her.

I sit forward in my seat and lock eyes with her. "I'm not trying for a better grade. What I'm telling you is the truth. Why don't you believe me?"

She lets out a sad breath, never breaking eye contact with me. "This is a highly unprofessional conversation, but if you must know." She clears her throat and looks off to the side for a moment before locking her gaze on me. "I'm not the kind of woman men or boys fantasize about."

What the fuck is she talking about?

"You've got to be kidding me. Don't play games with me. If you want compliments, I'll give you compliments." She shakes her head, and it's then I read in her eyes. She really doesn't believe me. "I don't know any sane male on the planet who wouldn't fantasize about you. Your body's smokin' and the red thing you've got going on drives me wild. There's no way a man hasn't said what a smoke show you are."

She looks down at her lap and then back to me. "Most men find that I'm too curvy. I won't lie, though. I've had compliments, but they were fueled by alcohol and not truth."

"Then those men are stupid because they don't know what they're talking about. Your body is what a woman's body should look like. I want nothing more than to…"

What the fuck am I saying?

How did we go from her scolding me for my stalker tendencies to me telling her what I picture when I'm jerking myself off to her?

"What do you want?" She asks, not so innocently.

It's then that I notice her chest is heaving and her cheeks are flushed, making me think she likes the words that have been tumbling out of my mouth.

"Are you sure you want to know? If you're just trying to get me to say things, so you can kick me out of class…"

"That's not why," she speaks softly. "Tell me what you want to do to me, Merrick."

"First," I say, and she raises a brow as if she's surprised I have multiple things I want to do with her body. She has no idea. "I want to bend you over your desk, push that skirt up over your hips, and fuck you from behind while I slap that sweet ass of yours until it's nice and pink."

She licks her red lips as she looks to the door.

Something brazen fills me, making me stand up and move over to her door and lock it. The whole while, I keep my eyes on her.

"You like what I want to do to you, don't you?" I ask as I take the few steps to her desk and walk around it. Gripping the back of her chair, I spin her around and look down at her. I fan my knuckles across her pink cheek and watch as her blush travels down her neck and into her shirt.

"If you don't want this to happen, you need to say something now because, in two seconds, I'm going to have you exactly the way I want you."

I wait. Longer than two seconds gave for her to say something. For her to tell me to leave her office and never come back, but the only thing she does is look at me with lust swimming in her chocolate-colored eyes.

I can't hold back another moment and take control of the situation.

"Stand up," I order. The moment she's on her feet, I press the palm of my hand between her shoulder blades until her chest is to her desk. I square myself behind her as I run my hands up the outside of her thighs and slowly start to push her skirt up and over the curve of her hips.

Now it's my turn to lick my lips. She's got on a tiny scrap of fabric between her legs that reveals the plump expanse of her ass. I want to lean down and bite it as much as I want to see my handprint on it.

Hooking my fingers into the strings that hold her underwear together, I pull them down her shapely legs and tap her leg for her to step out of them. Without thinking, I stuff her underwear into the front pocket of my jeans.

Her entire body is moving up and down as she breathes heavily, either from the excitement of what I'm doing or because she's scared of being caught. Maybe both.

Leaning down, I run my hands over her ass and up her spine. "This is your last chance to tell me to stop."

Not only does she not tell me to stop, but she wiggles her ass against my dick, and I swear I'm close to busting through my zipper.

Unable to take the torture any longer, I unbutton and unzip my jeans and push them and my boxers down enough to let my cock free. Pre-cum drips from the tip as if he's crying from being let out of his prison.

I run my cock along her crack and through her juices as I pull a condom out of my wallet. Thank fuck, I'm prepared. She's fucking soaked for me, and it's a heady feeling knowing I made her this way. I want nothing more than to feel her without any barriers, but I'm not going to tempt fate twice in one night and sheath myself.

Gripping her hip with one hand and tilting her ass up to me, I line myself up at her entrance and thrust inside. I give her a moment to adjust to my size and then let loose.

With each slam of my hips into her over and over again, my

hand connects with her ass. I growl, loving the sound of our skin slapping together and seeing my handprint on her pristine skin, knowing that I've marked her as mine.

Being inside of her is like heaven and hell all at once. Her pussy is so hot and tight, and I know the instant I'm inside of her, she's ruined me for all other women.

Roxie pants, and her hands clutch the edge of the desk as if her life depends on it as I rock into her over and over again.

"Fuck, you feel like nothing I've ever felt before. I could stay buried inside of you for the rest of my life."

Unable to hold back much longer and wanting Roxie to come before I do, I press my front to her back, pulling almost all the way out, and then slowly slide back in only to change it up. Taking two fingers, I rub slow circles around her swollen clit and feel her walls start to flutter around me.

"That's it," I murmur in her ear. "Come for me. I want to feel you milk my cock."

"Yes," she answers breathlessly, pushing her hips back in time with mine. "More," she begs, and it's like music to my ears.

Never in my wildest dreams did I think she would feel like nirvana at my fingertips.

When we're both close to exploding, I bury my face in the crook of her neck and take in her vanilla and honey scent. She smells divine—like her usual self, but also with my scent mixed in.

Pinching her clit between my fingers, I bury myself deep and shoot my load inside the condom. Her walls clamp down on me and don't let go.

She lets out a sob as she continues to milk me of every last drop. Bringing her down gently, I glide in and out of her at a leisurely pace, not wanting our first time together to ever end.

Only once she's spent on her desk do I pull out and place kisses up the column of her neck. Wrapping my arm around her, I pull her up and spin her around to face me.

Dipping down, I take her mouth in a searing kiss, unable to get enough of her. When we pull apart, her red lipstick is smeared, and she's never looked more perfect.

It's then I notice all the papers covering her floor. After tucking myself back inside my jeans, I bend down to clean up the mess we made.

When I stand back up, I find Roxie straightening out her skirt. She keeps her head down as if she can't look me in the eye. "Thank you, Mr. Landry. I hope you have a good weekend."

9
———

FOR A MOMENT, I FALTER. WHAT THE HELL? DID SHE seriously dismiss me like that? If anyone in this room is going to do a wham, bam, thank you, ma'am, it's going to be me, and that sure as fuck isn't going to happen. Not now after I've finally been inside of her and experienced the ecstasy that's between her legs.

When she turns around and notices I'm still standing in her office, her cheeks pink, and she looks to the messenger bag she's packing up.

"Can I help you? You got what you wanted, and now you can go on your way." Her voice is stiff and sad.

"Who said I got what I wanted? Because I know I sure as fuck didn't. I'm not sure I could ever get enough of you," I admit freely. Maybe if she realizes this isn't a one-off, she'll open up to me.

"Mr. Landry—" she starts, but I interrupt her. While I once thought it was hot, her calling me Mr. Landry, now I see it as a deflection. She's trying to make it all about business and nothing personal, and I don't like that. Not at all.

"For fuck's sake, call me Merrick. I've been inside of you. The least you can do is call me by my first name," I growl, unable to control my irritation.

She looks away and blushes again. With the way she's acting, you'd think she was a virgin before I slipped inside of her. I know for a fact she wasn't.

I'm not sure how to get through to her, so I decide maybe an ultimatum will work.

"Tell me that wasn't one of the best sexual experiences of your life, and I'll walk out that door, and I'll stop..." I can't say wanting her because I know what will never be the case. "Pursuing you."

Roxie opens her mouth and then promptly shuts it as her big brown eyes stare up at me. It's then I know she can't. It was just as good for her as it was for me.

"That's what I thought. Let's not play games here. It's beneath us."

"Mister," she starts but stops herself. She flops down in her chair and buries her head in her hands. "Merrick, this most certainly isn't a game. Do you realize my career is at stake here?"

"I know," I say softly, making my way around her desk and crouch down beside her. I run my hand down her hair that cascades down her back. It's so soft, and as my hand makes another sweep, the smell of vanilla springs free. "We can be discreet, and no one will ever find out."

When she lifts her head, her brown eyes hold so much

sadness in them it hurts to look at them. "You don't know what you're asking."

"Maybe I don't, but I know what I want, and I won't stop until I get it."

Her hands come up to rest on my chest. "I thought you already got what you want?"

"If that was the case, I'd already be gone. I want more with you. I have so many more fantasies I want to make a reality."

Again, she blushes, and I decide it's my new favorite color next to the signature red she wears on her lips.

Roxie Hart comes off as a strong woman, but for some reason, there's also a weakness, and I plan to do everything in my power to help make her stronger.

"Meet me this weekend. Tomorrow. We can drive down to LA, get a hotel, and fuck on every surface, and no one will be the wiser."

Looking at me, she gives me a sad smile. "I wish I could, but I can't. Right now, my brother can't be left alone for that long."

Tired of crouching by her side, I stand, pick her up in my arms, and then sit in her chair with Roxie on my lap. Taking her hand in mine, I rub soothing circles onto the back of her hand.

"What happened to your brother?"

"He got hurt, and now he's in both physical and emotional pain. It took me so long to convince him to stay with me that I can't leave him alone now. He thinks I don't know the amount of pain he's in, but I see what he's trying to hide. No one should go through what he has." Wetness fills her eyes as she bites her bottom lip. Every time up until now, it has been sexy as hell watching her bite down on her plump lip, but not now. Not when I know she's doing it to keep from crying.

"I won't ask you again to leave your brother, but surely we can still find a time to meet up this weekend. I can come to you." I barely get the words out before she's shutting me down.

"No," she jumps in my lap, looking extremely uncomfortable. "You can't. My brother can't know."

I'm not going to lie, her words hurt, but I'm not going to give up. I can't. Every fiber of my being is calling to make her mine, even if I have to put up with a little pain to get her there. Still, knowing she's ashamed of what was, hands down, the best experience of my life doesn't sit well with me.

"He can't know. Otherwise, he'll think I'm not living my full life while trying to take care of him. If he thinks I'm holding back from doing things in order for him to not be alone, he'll pack up and leave." She hangs her head. "He's not ready yet."

While I don't like the thought of hiding in the shadows, I understand. We can't get caught, and we can't go to either of our houses. That doesn't leave many places for us to meet up.

"We'll figure something out. Don't cut me out of your life yet." Grabbing a piece of paper off her desk, I scribble down my phone number and hand it to her. "Here's my phone number. When you can get away, call me with a time and a place, and I'll be there."

She stares down at the paper for a long moment, and for a minute, I think she's going to crinkle up the paper and throw it away, but eventually, she tucks it into her bag. "Now, I really should be going. I need to get home to take my brother to therapy."

She must see the question on my face because she answers me.

"If I don't take him, he won't go. I hate talking bad about him because I love him, but he's so depressed it's difficult to get him out of the house."

"I'm sorry you're both going through this. I wish I could help," I tell her honestly. If I could befriend him, I would.

"Thank you. I bet he'd like you, or at least he would if he was his normal self." She stands and puts her bag over her shoulder. "Have a—"

I don't let her finish her sentence. Grabbing her by the waist, I pull her flush to my body. My dick instantly responds to having her crushed against him. Dipping down, I crush my mouth to hers. I need one more taste to last me until I see her again.

When my tongue sweeps inside, Roxie moans. Her hands grasp onto my biceps and then move up to my shoulders and back.

A loud noise out in the hall has us jumping apart. Roxie's eyes are wide as she pants, trying to catch her breath while I stand as still as a statue trying to listen if someone's out there.

It isn't until now I realize how difficult it's going to be to keep whatever this is under wraps. While fucking her in her office was a fantasy, if we continue, it can also be the nail in the coffin forcing everything I've wanted to come to a screeching halt.

Taking her hand in mine, I give it a squeeze before I bring it up to my mouth and kiss her knuckles. "Good night, Roxie. I hope to hear from you… *soon.*"

She doesn't respond. Instead, she stares at me with something like wonder in her eyes as I open her door and make sure the coast is clear. Once I make sure there's no one out there, I turn and take her in. Her cheeks are flushed, lipstick smeared, hair a mess, and clothes rumpled. Roxie Hart looks like what wet dreams are made out of.

With that thought, I leave before I have to take her again.

10

———

Tapping my pen, I flip my phone over to look at the time to see it's been only five minutes since I last looked. It feels like it's been so much longer. I've waited all weekend for Roxie to call or text me, and it's been radio silence. If I knew where she lived, I'd be outside her house seeing what the hell she's up to because it certainly isn't me.

I know she didn't promise me anything, but I thought she was going to call. Now it seems like she was just trying to placate me to get me out of her office.

Little does she know that once Monday morning rolls around, I'm going to be waiting for her. Ready to pounce.

Hitting play on my phone, The Weeknd's Can't Feel My Face starts to play. I keep turning the volume up until I can't hear myself think any longer. I need to get Roxie out of my head and focus on my homework. I can't let her derail my academic career, no matter how much I want her.

Twenty minutes later, once all thoughts of my chemistry

teacher are out of my head, my phone starts to ring with an unknown number. My heart rate picks up at the thought it could be Roxie's number flashing across my screen.

I scramble none too smoothly to pick up my phone and almost hit decline instead of answer as I grab it. I'm all but panting as I answer hello.

"Merrick?" her voice is soft and unsure.

"Roxie?"

"I'm sorry it took me so long to call you. It hasn't been a good weekend, and when I realized I wouldn't be able to get away, I thought I should call you. Are you busy?"

Is she only saying she can't get away because she doesn't want to?

"My brother," she starts, her voice cracking. "I had to take him to the hospital, and we've been here ever since."

I almost ask if he's okay, but obviously, he's not. Otherwise, he wouldn't be in the hospital.

"Is there anything I can do for you?" I ask, even though I know there's nothing within my power to help either of them. I'm not sure what exactly is wrong with her brother, but I have a feeling it has to do with his limp.

"That's very sweet of you to ask, but unfortunately, no. Anyway, I wanted you to know I'm not standing you up. Although, I don't know why we should meet again." She says the last part so quietly into the phone I barely hear her. If I wasn't so attuned to her every nuance, I would have missed it.

"Why?" I growl. "Don't lie to yourself and pretend you don't feel the connection we have together."

"It was nice," she says just as quietly as before.

Is she in the room with her brother?

"I'm not talking about the sex, Roxie. I'm talking about everything else between us." I can't put it into words the way she makes me feel, but I know she feels it too.

"I… I… I need to go. There won't be a class tomorrow. I'm going to send out a message letting everyone know it will be canceled. Maybe I'll see you on Wednesday. Goodbye, Merrick."

Before I can question her or even say goodbye back, she hangs up, leaving me in the dark once again.

THE NEXT FEW DAYS ARE THE LONGEST OF MY LIFE. I GET up bright and early on Wednesday morning to check my email to see if Roxie's canceled class again, but there's nothing there. I'm not sure I wouldn't have stormed the hospital looking for her if we didn't have class again.

If I knew where she lived, I'd be camped out in front of her house, waiting for her to get home.

Wanting to get a word with her before class starts, I get dressed and make my way to campus. I arrive so early the doors to the building aren't even unlocked yet. At least I know I'll catch her on the way in.

Sitting down on the closest bench, I wait for someone to unlock the doors. The sky is still dark, and the morning dew is still on the grass as I pull out my notebook, hoping I can get some studying in. I haven't been able to concentrate much, but now that I know I'll see Roxie, I need to get my head on straight.

There's pressure on my shoulder as I crack open my eyes and am met with the early morning sun.

"Dude, what are you doing sleeping outside?" Walker asks as he towers over me.

I look around to find the campus is buzzing with students. I pull out my phone to check the time to see I'm thirty minutes late to my class.

How the hell did I fall asleep?

Standing abruptly, I grab my backpack and throw it over my shoulder. "I've got to go. I'm late for class."

"No, shit," he laughs but then sobers quickly. "Seriously, are you okay?"

"I'm fine. I got here early and fell asleep," I say as I start to walk away.

He tips his chin up at me. "That's why you shouldn't take early morning classes."

He knows I didn't have a choice, and I also don't comment on him being up early. It's a rarity unless he hasn't gone to sleep yet.

"Is everything good with you?" I call back, opening the building door.

He gives me a chin nod. "It's all good."

"We'll catch up soon, but I've really got to get to class."

He gives me a knowing look but doesn't say anything. Instead, he gives me a dismissive wave and starts to walk off toward the music building, where he spends most of his time.

I race inside and pull open the door to class to have everyone's eyes turn to look at me, including Roxie.

"Nice of you to join us, Mr. Landry. Now, if you could take your seat so I can continue, I'd appreciate it." Her normally soft voice has steel in it this morning. It makes me wonder if things are still not going well for her brother.

With only fifteen minutes left in the class, I try to scribble everything on the whiteboard down in my notebook and barely manage it before class is dismissed.

"Can I see you for a minute, Mr. Landry?" Roxie asks as I start to put away my notebook.

I nod, wanting nothing more than a few minutes alone with her. We stand silently until the class is empty, and when the last student files out, I move to touch her, but she backs away like I have the plague.

"Not here. Not now," she says firmly. "If you can't take what I have to lose seriously, then don't bother meeting me tonight at the park."

The park?

Is this her way of giving us a place to hook up?

"I do," I promise her. "But I've been miserable not being able to see or touch you."

"I don't know what I'm thinking," she says under her breath.

Her words piss me off, and it takes everything within me to hold back from saying something that could damage us before we even start.

"Tell me something. If you felt this way about a man who isn't your student, would you put up this much of a fight?"

"But you are my student, Merrick. When you say things like that, it makes me realize how young you are and why I should have nothing to do with you."

My nostrils flare, and I grind my molars as I try to rein in my emotions. When I can finally speak without yelling or getting in her face, I speak. "You didn't answer the question."

"No, I wouldn't, but that doesn't matter because the simple truth is, You. Are. My. Student." She pointedly says each word as if she wants to burn them into my brain.

"Not always. Once the semester's over, I'll no longer be in your class. It's only for a few months."

"We don't have time to discuss this right now. Meet me at the park tonight at five-thirty, and we'll talk then. I'd ask if you know my car, but obviously, you do."

She's so angry, and it's unlike her. I chalk it up to worrying about her brother.

"I'm sorry if I upset you. It wasn't my intention." Raising my hand, I lightly brush my fingertips over hers. "I'll see you tonight, Ms. Hart."

For the rest of the day, I have a spring in my step, and I feel lighter than I have in days. Tonight, I'll finally get to spend some time with Roxie.

11

———

Pulling up to the park, I find it deserted of all other cars except Roxie's. While I knew where the park was, I'd never been to it, and when I look around, I find it's a little run down and sad.

I park beside her and get out, expecting her to get out of her car as well, but instead, she continues to sit.

Opening the passenger door, I sit down in the seat to find her on the phone with a pinched look on her face. I can hear the person on the other end of the line yelling, but I can't make out what she's saying.

"I've got to go now, Mother." She pauses and listens to something else. "If you cared so much, maybe you should think about visiting your son. Don't put me in the middle because you won't like which side I take." Another pause, and then she says. "Goodbye."

She hits the end button on her phone and then throws it on her dashboard. She stays stiff as a board while she stares out of her windshield like the outside world has all the answers to her problems.

Taking her hand in mine, I start to rub circles on the back of her hand. "I take it you're not close to your mom."

"Not close would be an understatement. I'm not even sure why I answered the phone." It's then she finally looks at me, and I can see the anger and sadness reflecting in her eyes. "Maybe tonight isn't such a good night."

"I'm happy to sit here and listen and talk. Get whatever you need off your chest." She looks surprised by my words, but I mean every one of them. "If I could, I would take away all of your pain and stress."

She leans back into her seat and rolls her head to look at me. "You really are a sweet guy, but I don't want to talk about it. All I want to do is forget the last few days ever happened."

I know exactly what to do to make her forget.

"I think I can be of assistance. At least for a little while." Her car isn't big, but I can make do with what I got. "Why don't you come over here and sit on my lap."

There's a brief hesitation before she starts to move. Holding my hand up, I stop her. "First, take off your panties."

Not wasting any time, she slowly wiggles out of her dark red lacy underwear and takes them down her legs and over the heels of her red high heels. She throws them to the floor before she gets up on her knees and then moves to straddle me in the passenger seat.

"Like this?"

Gripping her waist, I let my fingers dig into her supple flesh as I hold her over my straining cock. "Just like this.

You're perfect. Now, why don't you help me out with my zipper."

She deviously smiles as she pulls back just enough to give herself room to unbutton and unzip my pants and pull the crown of my head out so that it's laying flat against my stomach.

"All the way out, baby. I want to make you feel better."

Her eyes light up at my words. I raise my hips and pull my pants and underwear down to mid-thigh.

Wasting no time, Roxie grabs the condom from my hands and makes quick work of covering my shaft with the latex barrier. Grasping me in her small hand, she places me at her entrance. Agonizingly slow, she lowers herself down until she's fully seated. Already I can feel her slick juices as our thighs touch. It feels good to know she wants this just as much as I do.

She starts to rock and moan, letting out a keening sound that nearly has me releasing on the spot. "Oh, God."

With her hands on my shoulders, Roxie starts to ride me with unbridled passion. Her pussy is so wet and hot. "Fucking hell, how do you feel better today than you did last time?"

Needing to suck on her succulent tits, I grip her shirt and tear it open. Buttons fly all over the car, but neither one of us cares. My hands weigh her breasts before pulling down the cups and letting them all free. Her smooth, creamy skin is begging to be marked to show everyone who she belongs to.

Taking her mocha-colored nipple into my mouth, I suck and nibble. Going back and forth between the two as if I can't decide which tastes better, I leave little marks for her to remember me by until we can meet again.

"Merrick," she cries out my name as her walls start to flutter around me. I grit my teeth, wanting to prolong the moment longer.

"Touch yourself," I demand, even though I know it will bring me over the edge.

She stops moving for a moment and looks down at me, unsure.

"You've got no reason to hide from me. You're the sexiest woman I've ever laid eyes on."

At my words, her eyes flare with lust as she takes two fingers and starts to rub her clit with them. Immediately she starts to buck in my hold, and I know she's close.

"That's the hottest fucking thing I've ever seen. Now let me taste you," I growl.

She brings her fingers up, and I dive for them, unwilling to wait to have her taste on my tongue. She's divine. We really need to find a place where I can go down on her because I need to spend at least an hour between those legs of hers. I want to feel her legs tremble as I bring her closer and closer to the edge.

Swirling my tongue around her fingers, I let them go with a pop and smile. "You taste better than anything I've ever tasted in all my life. I want to feast between your legs for days on end."

My hips rise as I pull her down, her ass slapping against my legs and our heavy breathing filling the small space of her car, making the windows fog up.

Heat shoots down my spine, and my balls start to tingle. "Touch yourself again, baby. I'm close, and I want you to come with me."

This time she has no hesitation as she touches herself. She arches her back and throws her head back as her walls clamp down on me, bringing me over the edge.

Gripping her hair, I pull her to me and take her mouth, swallowing down her scream as she comes undone on top of me. Wrapping my arms around her, I pull her down one final time and spill into the condom, wishing I was releasing inside of her.

We sit with her on my lap, her head on my shoulder and my arms holding her tight for long minutes as we try to calm our breathing. Roxie's the first to break the connection. She sits up and looks down at me with a smile on her face.

"That was unexpected," she finally says.

"Was it?" She nods but doesn't say more. "Why was it unexpected?"

Her thumb rubs along my bottom lip. Her eyes following her movements. "I didn't think it would be that good again. I thought last time might be a fluke, but now…" she trails off and starts to remove herself from my lap.

I hold her in place, liking the way she feels on me. "That's us. I think it will only get better with time."

Her hand comes up and cups my cheek. "I could easily get addicted to you, Merrick Landry."

"That's a good thing since I'm already addicted to you." I suck her bottom lip for a moment before I sit back. "While this was amazing. We're going to have to find someplace else to meet up."

"What's wrong with my car?" She smirks.

"For one, I want to lay you out before me, so I can taste every inch of your soft skin."

"And the other," she prompts.

"This feels cheap, and you're better than that. You deserve more than having to hide."

"But that's what we have to do. No one can know. If I get caught…" she trails off and hardens her jaw.

"I know, and trust me, I don't want that to happen, but surely there are better places than your car."

"We've always got my office."

But in her office, I can't make her scream my name. I guess beggars can't be choosers. In this case, I'll take it whenever and wherever I can to spend time with her outside of class.

"I really should be going. My brother will be looking for me soon." I must not have hidden the pain on my face as well as I thought I did. Holding my face in her hands, she kisses my forehead, my eyes, and then my nose before kissing each side of my mouth. "I wish I had more time, but this is the way my life is. If you can't handle it, I suggest we stop now before one of us gets hurt."

If we stop now, I'm already going to get hurt, but she's right. If I can't handle what she's giving me, we'll never make it through this. She may think all I want to do is fuck her, but she'd be dead wrong. I want to make Roxie mine until the end of time.

"I can handle it, and if I can't, I'll let you know because I'm not ready to let you go yet, Roxie."

"Then this is how it has to be. I wish we had more time." The look on her face screams that she's sincere.

"When can we meet again?" When she furrows her brows like she's going to turn me down, I blurt out, "It doesn't have to be sex. I'd be happy to spend time with you any way I can."

She nods and gets off my lap. I already miss her heat and weight, but I know I can't pull her back. Her brother needs her, and I can't be selfish.

After pulling her skirt down, she grips the steering wheel like her life depends on it. Her knuckles are white, and I can see the muscles in her arms flex as she stares straight ahead for a moment. At first, I think this is her dismissal of me, but then she turns to look at me with determination in her eyes.

"Meet me tomorrow at five. That's when my last class gets out. We can call you something like my teacher's assistant, but more like grading papers and whatnot. It will give us more time together without looking suspicious. Does that work for you?"

"I'll do whatever it takes to spend more time with you." I don't even care that I sound desperate. It's the truth. I am. I want to spend every second with her that I can.

"Good, I'll see you tomorrow evening."

This time I know I've been dismissed. Each side of her turns me on. I like it when she's shy, but I like it even more when she's assertive and knows what she wants. I want to bring more of that out in her.

Tucking myself back into my jeans, I lean over the console and slide my tongue inside her surprised mouth. I only taste her for an instant, knowing it will have to be enough to last me until I see her again.

"Until tomorrow."

12

I wasn't lying yesterday when I said I wanted to spend time with Roxie, and it didn't have to be sex. Not that I'd mind if it ended up with her body writhing underneath mine, but I want to get to know her and for her to know me. For her to trust in the way I feel about her.

Unsure if she's actually going to give me work to do just so I can spend time with her, I bring my laptop along with me as I walk from my apartment to the science building.

It's then I realize I never got back to Walker. I've been so consumed with all thoughts of Roxie, and I've let our friendship fall to the wayside. It's even worse since I know he won't be around much longer once Titan Records signs him and the rest of the guys in Crimson Heat.

Pulling out my phone, I dial Walker to check in.

"Hey, man," he answers on the second ring. "Give me a minute to get somewhere quiet."

A few seconds later, he comes back on the line. "What's up?"

"Nothing. I realized I never talked to you again after you found me sleeping outside."

He laughs at that. "Never thought I'd see the day."

"It wasn't on purpose. I hadn't been sleeping well, and then when I got to the building, the doors were locked, so I sat down and fell asleep. I can't believe no one from my class woke me up. The assholes."

"It's not their job to make sure you get to class. Besides, they're probably tired of you making eyes at your teacher," he chuckles down the line.

"How did you know that's the class?"

"Because why else would you get there early."

True. Only Roxie can get me out of bed at the ass crack of dawn.

"So, how is operation bag the teacher going?" He asks curiously.

It's crass, but I don't fault him. He doesn't have any idea how I feel about Roxie. It feels good to be able to talk to him about her. "I'm on my way to see her now. You know we have to do the whole 'hide we're together because I'm her student and she's my teacher' thing. We haven't been able to spend much time together outside of class."

"Your powers of persuasion must be fading. The Merrick I used to know could make any girl do anything he wanted," he laughs like it brings him great happiness.

"Well, she's a woman and not a girl and has real-world problems. It's not that her daddy will ground her if she's caught out late or in the backseat with a guy." I defend myself.

"Alright, chill out, man. I'm just giving you shit. I know how it is. Who would have ever thought when we were younger that we'd both be interested in older women?"

Not I. Before Roxie, older women never appealed to me, and now all I can see is her.

"How's it going with Penelope?" I'm close to the science building, which means I'll have to get off soon, but the last time I talked to him about her, he seemed torn up about it.

He lets out a defeated sigh. "She's still pushing me away, saying it was a mistake and it can't happen again. Who the fuck is going to find out? It's not like I'm fucking my teacher."

"Very funny, asshole. One thing I know from talking to Roxie is she's scared of losing her job. Since we can't meet at her house or mine, that only leaves us places where it would be easy to get caught. But I understand her concerns, and maybe if you express that you understand Penelope's, it will work in your favor."

Walker hums on the line. "You might be right. All I keep saying is it will be fine, but if I acknowledge her fear, maybe she'll stop pushing me away."

Maybe.

He clears his throat, and the moment he speaks, I can tell he's got a big-ass grin on his face. "She said they're working on a contract now. Can you believe it?"

"I never had a doubt. You're crazy-ass talented, man. I always knew you were going places. Just don't forget me once you're famous."

"As if I'll ever forget you and your scrawny ass."

"Scrawny ass? You're lucky you said that over the phone and not to my face because I'd kick your ass. You better hope I don't see you walking on campus, or I'm going to pound your ass to the ground."

"Okay, tough guy. I get it. You *think* you can beat me up. But did you hear me when I said I'd never forget you?"

"I did," I answer reluctantly.

"And we'll always be friends. You don't need to worry about it. If my head ever gets too big, you can just remind me of all the shit you have on me."

We both laugh at that. He knows I'll have no problem calling him out or bringing up one of the thousand stupid things he did growing up.

Fuck am I going to miss him.

"Let's hang out soon, okay? Get a drink or something," I lean against the brick building.

"Deal. I've got to get back to practice, and you've got to get to your woman."

A smile spreads across my face at his words. I love the sound of Roxie being my woman.

"Text me later and let me know when you're free."

"Done. Later," he calls before hanging up.

Willow Bay won't be the same without Walker Pierce or Crimson Heat.

I take the back doors that lead to the teachers' offices, and the second I step inside, Roxie is coming out of the teacher lounge area with a water bottle in hand.

"Hey," she says quietly. "You look…" she tilts her head to the side, accessing me. "Happy and sad. How is that possible?"

"I just got off the phone with Walker. He thinks he'll be signing a contract soon, and that means he'll be leaving Willow Bay."

She places her hand on my arm, and her eyes fill with understanding. "And you."

"It's okay. I always knew it would happen, but I guess I wasn't as prepared as I thought I was."

"We never are. If you want to skip tonight, you can."

Is she crazy?

There's no way in hell I'm passing up the opportunity to hang out with her, even if it is to grade papers.

"You can't get rid of me that easily. What do you have for me to do?"

"I thought you could help me catch up on some grading. I hate falling behind since I know students like to see how they're doing, but with Declan in the hospital, I couldn't help but fall behind."

I hold my arm out for her to go ahead of me. "Put me to work then."

"You may regret those words. I have an awful lot to grade."

I've always wondered why teachers give students so much homework when they have to grade it. I can't imagine having to grade hundreds of students' assignments.

"I have an answer key for you to go by. For this first set, it's as simple as right or wrong. Once you're through with this stack, let me know." She hands over a stack of papers that's at least two inches tall.

"How long does it normally take you to grade all these?" I ask as I flip through the papers. She seems to think I'll get through these and more when in reality, I'll be lucky to get through all of them by midnight.

She lets out a quiet laugh. "I know it may seem daunting right now, but once you get through a few of them, you'll realize how fast you're going to finish."

I'm not sure I believe her, but I sit down across from her and lay the answer sheet next to the mile-high stack of papers to grade. "I'm taking it this is why teachers have assistants."

"They don't do everything, but yes, I wish the school would have given me advanced notice they were down TA's. Also, not many want to do it for the classes I teach."

I nod because I agree. I wouldn't want to assist in this, and I'm hot for her.

We're quiet for a long time as we both splash red ink onto paper and set it aside to start with the next. She's right, it does go quick, but it's still going to take a good amount of time to get through everything.

Without looking up, I decide now is the perfect opportunity to start getting to know one another. "Can I ask you something?"

When she doesn't answer, I lift my head to find her looking at me with unease written across her face.

"It's nothing bad," I laugh. She's looking at me like I'm going to make her give me a detailed account of when she lost her virginity.

"I guess, but if I don't like the question, I have the right not to answer."

"Fair, but I think you'll be okay. How old are you?"

She has a smile on her face as she says. "Hasn't anyone ever taught you it's not polite to ask a woman her age?"

"I've heard it a time or two," I chuckle. "But I thought that pertained to older women who don't want anyone to know their age. You're young. I mean, when I first saw you in front of the class, I thought you were the TA until you announced yourself as the teacher. How wrong I was." I can't help but shake my head, thinking back to that day. I was dumbstruck by this beautiful woman in front of me. "You don't look old enough to be a teacher?"

"I've always looked young for my age, but I am the youngest teacher here on staff."

"So there's nothing to be ashamed about."

She doesn't look at me when she says. "Except for the fact that I'm fucking my student when I know I shouldn't."

"If they knew what I feel for you, they'd make an exception." I understand the rules, but if they had any idea the feelings that course through my body because of her, they'd change their mind.

"No, they'll fire me and have you seek counseling."

The guilt written on her face tears me up inside, but I believe it's because she's fighting her feelings for me and doesn't believe mine for her.

"You didn't answer the question. How old are you?" I'm not letting her out of answering.

"Thirty," she blurts out.

She's older than I first thought when I laid eyes on her, but she's young. Yes, she's eight years older than me, but it seems that I have a new type, and that is older women.

"Are you thinking differently of me?" She asks, unease in her tone.

"Not at all. I mean, thirty makes sense when you think about it. I was actually thinking how it seems like I have a type."

"And what type is that, Mr. Landry?"

"Older women. To be more precise, one older woman who is the hottest fucking thing I've ever laid eyes on who likes to wear red lipstick, glasses, and high heels to match."

Her cheeks flush, and I watch it travel to her heaving breasts. "You're such a flatterer."

"Not really. I'm only telling you the truth as I see it. I'm sure you think I'm young," she nods at my assumption. "But I promise you, I'm not some naïve little boy. I know what I want, and this isn't some passing infatuation. The more I get to know you, the more I'm intrigued and want more of you and your time."

I let her read the sincerity of my words written on my face, and when she's done, we go back to grading papers. After a few minutes of silence with only the sound of our pens and paper, she clears her throat.

"Can I ask you a question?" Her eyes dart around the room.

"Anything." It pleases me that she wants to know more about me.

"What made you decide to be a chemical engineer?"

It's not what I thought she wanted to ask, but I answer anyway. I've got nothing to hide. "My grandfather died when I was young. A big company a couple of towns over was dumping their waste into the water, and he got sick. Since then, I've wanted to make our planet a better place. I asked what I could become to do just that, and after weighing my options, I decided to become an environmental engineer."

"I'm sorry to hear about your grandfather. That's terrible," she frowns from across her desk.

It really is. Luckily my grandmother sued them for every dime they had, and now the company is no more. I've never understood why companies think they can get away with fucking over the little guys. Especially when half the population was getting sick from their carelessness.

I give her a small smile because what else can I do?

"Where do you see yourself after you graduate?"

I want to say wherever she is, but I know that's not what she wants to hear. The truth is, I've been planning to stay here in Willow Bay, where I grew up and work at a local company, Enviro Corp. I've been interning there for the last two years during the summer, and they've reassured me there will be a position for me when I graduate.

"Here, actually. I'm going to work at Enviro Corp. I'm not sure if I'll always work there, but for now, that's the plan."

After a few more questions, we get back to work. These papers aren't going to grade themselves. I'm surprised when I finish the first set, and it's only been a little less than an hour.

"What's next?" I ask, and when she doesn't respond, I look up to find Roxie staring at me.

Her eyes are hungry and not for dinner. No, she wants me

more than she's ever wanted me before. I decide to give us both what we want.

"I think I'm in need of a little snack."

"Oh, well, we can take a break, and you can go to the vending machines."

"It's not food I want," I say as I stand and make my way around her desk. Kneeling before her, I turn her chair until she's facing me.

Running my hands up the inside of her legs, I push her legs open when I get to her knees. Her skirt hinders how wide I want her spread out before me. Sitting back on my heels, I order her to stand up. She does as directed, which makes me smile. I love how she's up for anything. Pushing her skirt up, I don't stop until it's bunched up at her waist. "Sit and spread your legs wide for me, pretty lady."

I realize then I should have removed her underwear while I had her standing, but I'm not going to let a scrap of fabric be my downfall. Instead, I hook my fingers into the drenched satin and push it to the side.

Her pussy is glistening, and my dick notices. He wants out of the confines of my jeans. But not now. I've been dying to taste her since she slipped her fingers in my mouth, and I tasted her juices.

Holding her legs open, I dip down and slide my tongue through her wet folds and let out a low growl. From this moment on, this pussy is mine. If anyone comes near it, I'll rip them to shreds.

Needing better access, I place one leg over my shoulder and use my fingers to open her hood. Starting from her opening, I lick her up and down and then swirl around her nub, causing her to buck up against my face.

Roxie's fingers tangle in my hair, pulling at the strands and guiding me to where she wants me the most. Slipping two fingers inside her core, I pump in and out while I suck and caress her clit with my tongue.

"Don't stop," she moans even as she presses herself further into my face.

I don't plan to stop, but I don't bother to tell her that. Instead, I add a third finger, stretching her, and just as her walls start to flutter, I crook my fingers inside her to touch the place I know will set her off.

Opening her up to me, I use my tongue to drive her over the edge. Her body starts to tremble around me, her walls pulling my fingers deeper inside, and that's when I strike. Biting down on her clit to bring a little bit of pain to her pleasure, Roxie cries out, and I have to place my hand over her mouth to keep her quiet. It gives me great satisfaction to see she's letting herself go, but at the same time, I know we can't be caught. If we were, I'd lose her.

When her cries become pants, I remove my hand. Pulling back, I kiss her inner thigh and slip my fingers coated in her juices into my mouth, and moan at the taste. I swear my eyes roll back in my head.

I move to stand, but she catches my hand. Her eyes are starry as she looks up at me. Her face is relaxed and sated.

"That was… wow. I'd ask where you learned how to do that, but I don't want to know."

The idea of Roxie being jealous of women I've previously

been with makes me want to beat my chest and howl at the moon.

"It's all you. I take my cues from your body and do whatever I can to bring you the most pleasure."

"I'm not sure I believe you, but I do like your answer." Her hands go to the button on my jeans, but I stop her. Even though I'm dying, I didn't go down on her so she'd return the favor.

"You don't need to do that."

"But what if I want to? I can see how hard you are through your jeans."

"Make no mistake, I want you, but you don't owe me anything. It was my pleasure having my head between your legs."

She licks her red lips, and I can't help imagining having her lipstick staining my cock. I start to unzip my jeans when there's a knock on the door.

I don't think I've ever moved faster in my life as I run around the desk and sit back down in the chair I previously occupied. I pick up one of the assignments I graded and stare at it as Roxie calls for whoever it is to come in.

It's not until that moment, I wonder if she's righted herself, but then I shake my head. Of course, she did. She's not going to call someone into her office with her skirt pulled up to her waist.

"Ah, Jeremy. How are you today? I noticed you weren't in class," she gives him a tentative smile from across the room.

I turn to look over my shoulder at this Jeremy guy and realize he's in my class. He sits a few seats down from me.

"Ms. Hart, I was wondering if I could have a moment of your time, but I see you're busy. I can wait."

"That's okay. Merrick is helping me grade papers as we talk about his research paper, but I think we're done for the day." She looks at me and then tries to give me the same smile she gave him but fails. It's too bright, as are her eyes. Right now, she's definitely not looking at me like a student, but as someone she wants to have for lunch.

I stand, making the chair legs squeak against the floor. "Yes, thank you for talking me over those points. I think it will help me continue on with my paper."

"It's no problem at all. That's what I'm here for. In fact, I should be the one thanking you for helping me grade my papers."

"Is it extra credit?" Jeremy jumps in. "I'll help you one day, Ms. Hart."

"Maybe," she says, dismissing Jeremy. "Have a good night, Mr. Landry." She's looking down at her phone as I exit the room, and Jeremy takes my seat. I'm closing the door when I hear her say, "I hope ten minutes is enough. I really do need to be going."

I'm not sure if she's saying that for my benefit or if she really does need to leave, so I decide to wait for her meeting to end in case she wants me to wait.

Standing in the shadows, I'm about ready to give up when Roxie comes out of the building thirty minutes later. She's walking quickly and doesn't seem to notice me standing by her car until she's pulling out her keys.

"Merrick, what are you doing here?" She asks breathily.

"I was waiting for you. I wasn't sure if you wanted me to wait or…" I shrug, realizing now she probably didn't want me to wait.

"I'm sorry we didn't have more time, but I've got to get home. I hope you understand."

"I do," I say as I swallow the sudden lump in my throat, realizing I might be in way over my head with her. It's a strange feeling after what went down in her office. What if this is all it will ever be? Secret liaisons as she hides me from her world.

She steps forward and starts to lift her hand but then drops it. "Your words say one thing while your face says another."

"I'm just tired," I lie, not wanting to make her feel guilty for giving me only what she said she could.

"Well, get some sleep then, and I'll see you tomorrow night. How about we meet in the library?"

"Sounds good," I say, but I'm secretly wondering if she wants to meet there, knowing it will be next to impossible for us to hook up unless I get us a study room. She's turning me into a damn girl questioning everything and my feelings.

"Goodnight, Merrick."

Unable to say anything for the fear I might blurt out something that will cause her to run, I stand there and watch her go until I can no longer see her taillights. Only then do I head home.

13

NOVEMBER

EACH WEEK I RESERVE A STUDY ROOM FOR ROXIE AND ME at the library, and so far, it's our I guess you would call it our home away from home. It's the only real place we can get any privacy without fear of interruption. Every Thursday night, I get her all to myself for two hours, and it's the highlight of my week.

The only problem is Thanksgiving break is next week, and after that, the semester will soon end. I thought that once I'm no longer one of Roxie's students, she would be open to being seen out in public with me, but she wants to wait until the end of the school year. I'm not sure how we're going to be able to meet up when she's no longer my teacher.

"Why do you look so sad?" Roxie asks as she slips on her high heels.

She asks like she didn't just drop a bombshell on me.

"I don't see us being able to spend much time together once this semester is over if you won't be seen with me in public."

She lets out a sigh as she sits down in the chair across the table from mine. "You were the one who thought everything would change because you'd no longer be in my class. I never told you I'd go out and hold hands with you in front of the student body. I can't risk my job."

But she's willing to risk me.

"How are we going to be able to spend time together?" I ask, sounding like a whiny bitch. When did I turn into the girl in this relationship? I fucking hate what she's turned me into.

"Merrick, just because you're not in one of my classes doesn't mean we can't still meet here."

I guess she's right, but I don't want to hide anymore. Another six months feels like a lifetime.

"I'm sorry, but that's how it has to be," she says like she read my mind. "I'll have more free time during break. While I can't give you all my time, it will be more. That's something, isn't it?"

We might be able to spend more time together, only making my need for her more consuming once break is over, and then how will I cope when I can barely see her again?

"Where are we going to go when the campus is closed down? My roommates haven't decided if they're going home for the holidays or not, and we can't go to your house."

"They should. I'm sure their poor parents miss them," she says, dismissing my comment about her house.

Maybe. Or maybe their family is happy their messy children are finally gone—I know I'd be happy to have them gone for winter break.

"I can't say. We don't talk much. This is my first time living with them, and it's been an adjustment, to say the least." We don't talk about my roommates or her brother much because it only leads to how we're stuck to meeting each other in the library or in a dark parking lot somewhere.

"That bad, huh?"

"They're both disgusting pigs. It's like they thought they'd live with me for the cheap rent and hoped I'd clean up after them. Their bedrooms are biohazards. We'll be lucky to get our deposit back."

"Oh, I remember my college days. I had a messy roommate." She shivers, and not in a good way. "We had mice because she was so nasty. You don't have mice, do you?" She leans back in her chair, looking at me as if I might have a mouse in my pocket.

"Not that I know of, but we're probably not far from it. I can't wait until I don't have to have roommates any longer."

Although, I can think of someone I wouldn't mind living with. I bet she's tidy.

"Maybe you'll get lucky, and they'll go home," she pats my hand as she starts stuffing all of her things into her messenger bag.

"That's the only way we'll be able to spend time together. If not, it will be when school starts back again, and then who knows." I sound like a pouty baby, but I don't care. Tonight is not looking good for us and the status of our so-called relationship. It would be nice to see that it might bother her not to see me for almost a month and a half.

She stops packing up her things and looks at me. "I understand you're not happy, but there's nothing we can do about it. I warned you when we started this. To be honest, I didn't think it would go on as long as it has."

"And why's that?" I ask, barely keeping myself in check. From day one, I've been honest about my feelings for her.

"I thought you'd be tired of me already. I never thought it would lead past one encounter, but you surprised me."

"In a good way or a bad way?" I can't help but ask. If Walker could hear me now, he'd laugh in my face. Instead, he's off in LA recording his first album. He signed the dotted line, and Titan Records had them in LA before the ink was dry—and before I got a chance to say goodbye. Maybe I'll go see him during break and get my mind off my troubles here.

"If it wasn't good, I wouldn't be here right now. I wish things were different, but they're not, so we have to make do with what we have for the time being. Either that or call this off. You should think about how you want this to go. For now, I have to leave."

I would call it off if I wasn't so addicted to her.

She moves around the table and drops a kiss on my lips that's too short for what I want, but I have no say in the matter. Instead, I turn in my seat and watch her walk out the door—her ass sashaying in her sexy as sin skirt.

Since I have the room for another hour, I pull out my laptop and try to finish up my research paper for Roxie's class, but I can't concentrate. All I can think about is how I might not see the woman who's become an undeniable craving in my life for over a month, and even then, we'll still have to hide our relationship.

Some days it feels like we'll always be hiding in the shadows.

Pulling out my phone, I pull up Walker's number and call him. It rings and rings and rings. I don't think he's going to answer, but then at the last minute, he picks up.

"Hey, man. What's up?" Walker answers.

"Same old, same old, what's up with you?"

"Nothing much," he answers, and then it sounds like he covers up the phone and whispers something.

"I doubt that, man. You're a famous rockstar now." I kid him. He's not famous yet, but he will be as soon as his music hits the airwaves.

Walker lets out a bark of laughter. "You don't know how good it is to hear your voice. Today's been rough."

That makes two of us.

"It's good to hear yours as well. What's going on?" Walker's a pretty laid-back guy, so for him to say it's rough, it must be bad.

"Nothing we do pleases the record company or the producer today. They're pretty much threatening to send us home if we don't sound better."

I highly doubt they'd do that.

"We're taking a dinner break so we can put our heads back on straight. Can you believe that?"

"I don't know. Did you guys party too much last night?"

"Not me," he shoots back instantly. It still doesn't answer for the rest of the guys.

"Did she put a leash on you to keep you out of trouble?" It takes everything in me not to laugh when he makes a sound of displeasure.

"Can't leash what you don't own." He says it like it doesn't bother him, but I know better. He doesn't talk about women, and the fact that he talks about Penelope is all the proof I need to know she means something to him.

"How about you? How's your lady doing?"

I want to laugh at the absurdity that both of us want women we can't seem to have. "If you mean she wants to continue doing what we're doing, which is seeing each other maybe twice a week outside of class and continue hiding the fact that we're… I don't even know what, man, then it's going great."

"Damn, man, is she holding out on you?"

"No," I laugh, wondering why he asked that. "Why?"

"Because it sounds like you need to get laid."

I did, but it wasn't enough. It's never enough in the short time we have with each other.

"Fuck off, man. I get laid plenty." I don't need his shit.

"If that's the case, then what's the problem?"

Even before a word comes out of my mouth, I know I'm going to sound like some pussy-whipped douchebag. "I'm tired of sneaking around. I thought once I wasn't in her class anymore, we could, I don't know, be out together or some shit like that, but no. She wants to keep our relationship in a ten by ten-foot room in the library."

"Damn, man, is she ashamed of you?" He laughs, joking, but it makes me wonder if maybe Roxie is embarrassed by me. "Hey, don't start thinking that way. I was only kidding. There's no way in hell she's ashamed of you."

"I don't know. Maybe you're right. All I know is if my fucking roommates don't go home for break, I'm screwed."

"You mean you won't be screwed," he laughs, and it makes me smile even when I don't feel like it.

"Yes, asshole, that's what I meant."

"Why don't you come here for break? I'd love to see you, and you two could have some private time."

"I wish we could, but she can't. She takes care of her brother and can't leave him overnight." Which makes me feel guilty when I ask for more of her time.

"Sucks to be you then. Well, if the roommates don't leave and you won't be seeing your lady, why not come visit me? It would be nice to see a friendly face that isn't one of the three guys currently making my life difficult."

"I might just do that. Either way, maybe I'll at least make a day trip or make it an overnighter, so we can hang out."

"I'd like that. Just let me know when. Titan set us up in a pretty sick place here, and there's more than enough room for you to stay if you want."

"I'll take you up on that. I'm still a broke college kid until I start my job this summer."

"Fuck, I can't believe you'll be a working stiff in a few short months."

It doesn't seem real, but I'm ready, especially if it gets me closer to spending time with Roxie outside of school.

"Well, I can't believe you left without saying goodbye, asshole," I shoot back. This isn't the first time I've mentioned it, but couldn't he have stopped by on his way out of town at least? Instead, all I got was a text.

"Stop being a bitch about it. I let you know I left, and I knew we'd see each other again, just not when."

"Fucking hell, she is turning me into a woman. I feel like I'm always complaining about my feelings and shit like that lately. What's happened to me? The next thing I know, I'll be having my period."

Walker laughs long and hard. "You're pussy-whipped, plain and simple. It's up to you to do something about it."

"What can I possibly do?" Walker is the only one I can talk to about Roxie, and it helps we're sort of in the same predicament.

"Make her see what she's got."

That's his advice?

"You suck at this, you know?" I grumble.

"Sorry, I'm not a girl. This is the best you're going to get." He lets out an annoyed sigh and then a loud yell. "I've got it."

My brows pull together. "What's that?"

"What you can do to Ms. Teacher. You need to make her jealous. Make her realize that if she can't give you more than you're getting, you've got plenty of other options."

"That's got to be the—"

"Best idea ever," he interrupts. "Trust me, dude, it will work. Have my plans ever let you down before?"

"No, but I don't see how this is going to make her want to be to be with me." She already said she thought I would get tired of her. If I tried to make her jealous, it would only prove her point.

But I'm desperate enough to try just about anything to make Roxie step out from the shadows with me.

"I know you're thinking about it. Yes," he yells. "If you need more advice, call me since I give the best damn advice," he boasts. "But for now, I've got to go and eat before we have to head back inside the studio."

"Good luck tonight, and remember I'm always here for you," I tell him. He tried to help me, and I've been utterly useless in helping him.

"I know," he says. It feels like there's more he wants to say, but then there's someone yelling in the background. It sounds like Greer, but I might be wrong. "Talk later."

Now I just need to decide if I should listen to Walker and try to make Roxie jealous or wait and see how this plays out.

14

Roxie's red lips pout down at me. "I hate that you're going to spend Thanksgiving alone."

I want to say she could invite me to her place, but I know that's not an option.

Licking along her breastbone, I hover over her mouthwatering tit, wanting to take it into my mouth and mark her. Taking her pert nipple into my mouth, I suck hard and don't stop until she's writhing on top of me. Her slick cunt slides over my shaft, coating me in her juices.

I let her tit pop out of my mouth and smile up at her when she lets out a moan of disapproval. "I'll be fine. I'll order pizza and watch Willow Bay kick some football ass."

At least my roommates will be gone, and I'll have the whole house to myself for an entire week. I don't tell her I plan to clean the place up so that she can come over.

"Now, why don't you ride my dick and make me a happy man?"

Her red lips spread into a wide grin as she continues to rub herself all over me like a cat in heat. She wants to play, but I can't wait a moment longer to slip inside of her. When her opening runs over the tip of my cock, I grip her waist and thrust inside of her.

She looks down at me with wide and excited eyes. Her hands go to my shoulders to anchor herself as I piston my hips up, slamming into her tight cunt over and over again.

"Oh, God, Merrick," she chants as she places one hand on the roof of her car and grinds down on me, taking what she wants. Throwing her head back, she lets out a sultry moan that nearly has me unloading inside her.

Gripping her neck, I suck and nibble along the column of her slender neck. Watching her skin turn pink from my attention sets something primal off in me. I wish we had more room. Fucking someone in a car is hot once, maybe twice, but when it's one of your only options, it starts to feel limiting. Still, I wrap my arms around her and lay her down on the backseat. It's a tight fit, but I need more. Hooking her legs over my arms, I place one hand on the window and slam into her.

Each thrust is punishing as my thighs slap against her ass. The sound only makes me push harder. My breath is ragged, and it's the perfect accompaniment to her loud moans and the way she cries out as she starts to let go.

Her walls start to quiver and suck me in as I pull out. I want to give her the best fucking orgasm of her life. Ruin her for all other men and make it known no one will satisfy her the way I do.

Roxie's back arches, and that's when I strike. I slap her

pussy, and Roxie convulses underneath me. She yells so loud I'm shocked the windows don't shatter.

I slow my stride and wait for her to start to come down, and only then do I pick up my pace, drawing out her pleasure. My thumb moves to her clit, and I rub furious circles.

"Merrick, it's too much," she moans, her eyes rolling into the back of her head. "Please," she begs.

I'm not sure if she wants more or for me to stop, but either way, I continue rolling her sweet little nub with my fingers as I slam into her. Her walls never once stop fluttering and quaking around me. I can't imagine what it must be like for her because it's the best damn thing that's ever happened to my dick.

When I can't hold back any longer, I hike her leg up high and bury myself deep and spill inside of her.

Letting her legs down, I pull her up with me and sit her on my lap. I relax against the seat and enjoy the feel of Roxie's hot breath on my skin. It's not until she shifts, and my wet cock is trapped against my leg, that I realize I fucked her without a condom. I was too caught up with her teasing me.

"Roxie, baby," I run my hand down her damp back.

When she only makes a sound, I tangle my hand in her hair and pull her back to look at me. Her brows knit together as she looks up at me with sleepy eyes. "Is it already time to go?"

"Not yet." At least, I don't think so. "Baby, I… I'm sorry. I got caught up in the moment, and I didn't use a condom."

Her sleepy eyes stay trained on me as they trace over my face.

"I promise I'm clean. I haven't been with anyone else since —" I start until she stops me.

Placing her fingers over my mouth, she hushes me. "If I thought for one second that you had an STD, I wouldn't be fucking you. Condom or not. I'm on the pill. I have been since I was sixteen years old to regulate my periods."

That's a relief, but it was still irresponsible of me.

"I've never gone without one. I should have known it felt too good."

She smiles at me. "It felt better for you?"

I breathe out a laugh. "It was the single best experience of my life."

"Mine too," she nuzzles into my neck. "I thought you were going to fuck me to death. My orgasm…"

"Kept going and going," I finish for her. The way her pussy clamped onto my dick and didn't let go was what dreams are made of.

She kisses up my neck and to my ear. "I want to do that again."

"Oh, we'll most definitely do it again, and many times when you get back from your parent's house for Thanksgiving. We're going to take advantage of the time my roommates are away."

"I like the sound of that." She hugs me and snuggles closer. A flash of lights sweeps through the car windows, putting us on high alert. I hate that our moment is ruined by some outside force.

Roxie slips off my lap and onto the seat next to me and starts to dress. I wish I could keep her naked and under me for the rest of time, but I know I have to be patient.

My shirt lands on my face, and Roxie laughs. The sound is soft yet raspy. "I'm sorry. I thought you'd catch it."

"I was too busy daydreaming of having you naked and keeping you hostage, so I can admire your body."

Roxie shakes her head as if she doesn't believe me.

"I wish you saw yourself as I see you."

She stops getting dressed. She's only in her bra and panties, and she's the sexiest damn thing I've ever seen. I want to lick each inch of exposed skin. "And how is that?"

"Like what a real woman is supposed to be. Men don't like to fuck twigs. We want soft curves and something to hold on to."

She rubs her fingertip over my lips. "I like the way you think. I love my body, but I've never had anyone else love it. I've always been put down because of the way I look."

"I love your body. Each and every beautiful curve of it."

Luckily, her lips crash to mine before I can spill out how I love her just as much as I love her body.

15

"Guess what?" Roxie says, smiling up at me. I've never seen her so happy before.

"What?" I ask as I haul her through my front door. I shut and lock the door for good measure while keeping her in my arms.

"Declan is staying with my parents for a couple of days, and that means—"

"You can stay with me the entire time," I say, carrying her through the house and into my bedroom. I kick my door closed and lock it too, just in case.

"Something like that." Her hands cup my face, and she kisses both sides of my mouth. "You look good when you smile."

"You've given me a lot to smile about," my smile only widens at what this news means.

I know I should probably wine and dine her, but right now, I've got to fuck her. Later, we can order dinner and watch a movie or something like that, but right now, I need to celebrate the best way I know how—by fucking my woman.

Setting her down on her feet, I sit down on the bed. Pulling out my phone, I pull up Spotify, and Señorita by Shawn Mendes and Camila Cabello starts playing through my bedroom speakers. "Strip for me."

She starts to kick off her signature red heels, but I tsk. "Keep those on. I want you to wear them while your legs are up by my head."

Her eyes light up, letting me know she likes what I have planned. She slowly starts to unzip her skin-tight jeans and then shimmies out of them. She's got a black lace thong on that has me drooling to see what's underneath it. She has to step out of her heels because of her jeans but then quickly steps back into them.

Reaching for the hem of her white sweater, she pulls it up over her head, leaving her in only her bra, panties, and heels. The way she's standing in front of me, full of confidence, has my dick so fucking hard. Unclipping the bra from the front, her full, creamy-white tits spill out against the black fabric. She lets the bra fall to the floor, and when her fingers hook into her underwear, I know I won't be able to hold back much longer.

I pull my t-shirt by the neck and throw it to the floor and lift my hips to slip off my athletic shorts. I palm my erection and watch as she ever so slowly starts to drag her thong down her legs and kicks them to the side.

Her eyes are trained on what my hand is doing while she pulls her hair out of a ponytail, and she slowly lets it fall down around her shoulders. Then she shakes her hair out, and it covers the tops of her breasts. She licks her lips as her eyes follow my hand up and down.

Crooking my finger, I beckon her to me. "That is by far the best striptease I've ever watched. Now I want you on your knees and for those pretty red lips to wrap around my cock."

Roxie wastes no time as she sinks to her knees before me and removes my hands to replace them with her own. Her silky soft hands feel like heaven as they wrap around my length and start to pump up and down.

She smiles up at me mischievously, knowing exactly what I want. Lowering her head, she wastes no time as she takes my length into her mouth and starts to suck. I pull her hair back and out of the way so I can watch. I smile at the lipstick ring around my cock, knowing it's going to be completely red by the time she's finished.

Palming the back of her head, I press down. "Take all of me."

Roxie doesn't disappoint. She opens her throat, and I slide all the way in. I keep my hand where it is but let her control the pace. I'm not into forcing my dick down her throat or making her gag.

Her head starts bobbing to the beat of the song as she cups my balls and starts to roll them in her hand. When one finger moves further back, I let go of her hair and lay back. Sucking on my tip, she swirls her tongue along the underside and then slips her finger through my tight ring. When she hits my prostate, I explode in her mouth. Jet after jet shoots in her mouth, and she takes it all. When I'm done, she kisses the tip of my cock and then slowly crawls up my body.

Roxie kisses and licks my abs and the flat discs of my nipples before she's straddling me and rubbing her sweet, wet pussy on my cock. "That was so hot I almost came from listening to you."

Gripping her hips, I start to pull her up until I feel the wetness of her core on my chest. "Come sit on my face and let me taste your sweet pussy. It's been too long."

"I don't know," she looks unsure.

"Grab onto my headboard and let me do the rest. I need to eat you first."

Placing her hands on the headboard, she scoots up until she's hovering over me, and I can see how wet sucking my dick made her.

One swipe of my tongue through her juices and I moan, needing more. I lick and suck at her lips and dive into her hot pussy, fucking her with my tongue.

Above me, Roxie rocks back and forth on my face and lets out little gasps and moans that have my dick hard and weeping to be inside of her.

Opening her wide for me, I lave her clit with the tip of my tongue, making her legs start to shake. I smile and continue while slipping two fingers inside and pumping in and out.

Roxie's always been responsive to my touch and now is no exception. Her entire body starts shaking even as she rubs her pussy all over my face and calls out my name like I'm her own personal god.

Slipping out from under her, I cover Roxie's back with my front and slip inside of her tight heat. I know I won't last long as I fuck her through her orgasm, but I can't wait a second longer to be inside of her.

With each stroke, she rears back against me. I'm as deep as I can go as I hit her cervix. Reaching back, Roxie's nails dig into my leg, and the jolt of pain has me unloading.

I kiss the side of her neck as I slip out of her, and Roxie lets out a whimper. "Don't worry. There will be plenty more. I don't plan on getting much sleep while you're here." I love that she's as hungry for me as I am for her.

Flopping onto my back, I pull her down to rest at my side and wrap my arms around her. It feels so good to have her here in my arms for once. This is the way it should be.

Now that my dick isn't leading the charge, I ask. "Are you hungry? We can order in and rent a movie. Whatever you like."

"I'm starved. You made me work up quite an appetite," she hums against my neck.

Living in Willow Bay, we don't have a lot of options for takeout, but luckily if you're willing to pay a hefty price, there's a couple of the neighboring towns that deliver, and my first night with Roxie in my bed is a reason to splurge.

Pulling her on top of me, I relish the weight of her body and the feel of her breasts pressing into me. "What are you in the mood for?"

Hiking her leg up on my hip, Roxie nuzzles into me. "Indian sounds good."

It does, but I know for certain Willow Bay doesn't have an Indian restaurant, and I'm not sure if one of the other towns that do will deliver. Would Roxie be willing to go with me to pick it up?

"Hey," she calls quietly and runs her hand down my arm until she reaches my hand. Taking my hand in hers, she laces her fingers through mine. "What's got you tensing up?"

Looking up at the ceiling, I explain to her what I was thinking, ready for the rejection.

"You're right," she says, and I tense again, knowing I'm right that she doesn't want to be seen out with me. "Stop it," she scolds. "No, you're right in the fact that they don't deliver. I wasn't thinking, but if you're willing to drive, then I'll happily ride along." Letting go of my hand, she crosses her arms over my chest and places her chin on her hands to look up at me. "It's not like I think you have the plague or anything. If there were no repercussions to me... dating a student, I would happily be seen with you anywhere and everywhere, but that's not the world we live in."

"I know," I let a sigh. "But that doesn't mean I have to like it."

"I don't like it either, but it won't be forever."

It certainly feels like it. The closer we get to the end of the semester, the more I feel like we've got an expiration date.

16

JANUARY

THE TWO DAYS I SPENT WITH ROXIE IN MY BED AND IN MY arms over Thanksgiving break were the best and worst days of my life. They were only the worst because it caused me to want more from her, and since both my fucking roommates decided to come back to Willow Bay right after Christmas, I haven't had the house to myself.

Roxie and her brother went to see her parents for Christmas, and by the time they came back, my roommates were back as well. Since my family lives right outside of Willow Bay in Loganville, I came home to an empty house after spending the day with my family and no Roxie to enjoy it with. I could have stayed at my mom's, but the house felt too crowded with my brother and sister both home from school. It didn't help that my mom has been questioning me about whether I have anyone special in my life. I don't want to lie to her, but I also can't tell her the truth because then she'll want to meet Roxie.

With school out on break, Roxie and I have been reduced to parking lot meetups and only once or twice a week.

Sitting in my car, I watch as Roxie pulls into the parking lot of the deserted park. She quickly gets out of her car and slides into my backseat. I've made it as comfortable as possible by cleaning out the back and placing a blanket across the seats. It's not much, but how romantic can you make the backseat of a car?

"Hey," she grips my shoulders from the backseat. "I'm sorry I'm late. Declan and I had a fight, and it was hard to get away."

I open the driver's door and then get into the back with her. I barely sit down before she's in my lap and laying her head on my shoulder. My arms go around her and hold her to me.

"What was your fight about?"

"He's wondering where I've been going and why I have to go to the grocery store so many times when we have a kitchen full of food."

I hold my tongue, knowing I can't mention her telling her brother about us.

She lets out a frustrated puff of air. "Just say it."

"Say what?"

"What you want to say. I can feel that you have something to say."

She asked for it.

"Would it really be so bad if your brother knew? The semester's over, and I'm not going to be in any more of your classes. You can tell him I'm busy if you're worried that he'll want you to spend more time away from the house. I'm sure we can come up with something where you're not lying to him."

And I'm not your dirty little secret.

She's quiet for so long that I think she's not going to say any more on the matter or possibly fell asleep, but then her head pops up, and she smiles at me.

"You know what, I think you're right. I'll tell him that I'm seeing you, but that you have a very busy schedule. That should appease *him* and *you*."

The amount of happiness I'm feeling can't be explained. I actually feel like I might combust with the thought of her brother finally knowing about us.

Leaning forward, I take her bottom lip in between mine and suck before letting it go. "I think it will make your life a hell of a lot less stressful. I can also help you relieve a little of the stress you're feeling now."

"Is that right?" She bites her bottom lip that's still wet from only a moment ago. "How is your stress level?"

"Over the top, out of this world," I joke with her as I slide my hands up her thighs and under her skirt. "Have I ever told you how happy it makes me that you wear skirts most of the time?"

"Why do you think I wear them?" She wiggles her ass. My cock is rock hard and begging to be inside of her from the movement. "Now, if we could only figure out a way to make your dick as easily accessible, we'd be golden."

I like the way she thinks.

"Why don't you pull him out, so he can greet you properly? He's missed you," I say as I pull the fabric of her underwear to the side and slip one finger deep inside of her. I pull my finger out and suck her juices off as she hastily unzips my jeans and wraps her tiny hand around my shaft.

"Fuck, baby, I love feeling your hands on me almost as much as I love being balls-deep inside of you."

Never one to disappoint, Roxie rises onto her knees and places the tip of my cock at her entrance. I don't wait for her to sink down. I need her now. Thrusting my hips up, I slam into her from below.

Roxie groans out my name as she throws her head back.

Leaning forward, I kiss up her neck as she starts to move on top of me.

I pump faster, excited by the notion that this might be the last time we have to meet up in a parking lot and hook up in a car. Once her brother knows about me, I can go over to Roxie's house—a place I haven't been to yet.

I spill deep inside her, my hands cupping her tits and squeezing as I groan long and deep.

Roxie follows after, stilling above me, and bites her bottom lip as her pussy milks me of my essence.

"Wow, what got into you?" She laughs breathlessly.

I nip along her collarbone. "That we might not have to keep meeting up in parking lots."

"Hey, it's not like we can do this at my house while my brother is awake. That's… eww. No, we won't be having sex with him listening."

"I never said that," I laugh. "Do you want me to be there when you tell your brother?"

"Ah, no. I think that should be a private conversation between him and me."

"Okay," I hold my hands up. I'm not sure why it's such a big deal, but she knows her brother.

"He's just a little sensitive about the subject matter right now. He had a girlfriend before he graduated, and I thought they stayed together, but…" she shrugs. "I don't know what happened between them except that they're not together anymore."

"Being injured and broken-hearted can't be easy. It's nice that you care so much about him. I can say for certain that my little sister wouldn't spare my feelings. In fact, she'd probably rub it in."

"That's because she's a little sister and not a big sister. You wouldn't do that to her, would you?"

I might want to, but she's right; I wouldn't purposely hurt Avery or Maverick.

"You're right. I wouldn't," I admit.

Lifting her hand, she runs her fingertips along my jawline. "Why don't you talk about your siblings much?"

"We're not close. Never have been. But they are, even though it doesn't make sense with the age differences. I'm a year older than Maverick and four years older than Avery. He's a junior here, and I never see him. He's busy with football, and when I tried to ask him about it when I saw him at Christmas, he didn't want to talk to me about school or anything, really."

Roxie lays her head on my shoulder. "Declan and I haven't always been close, but once I graduated high school, something happened. I thought we'd grow further apart, but it was the opposite."

"Maybe the same will hold true for them once they're older. At least they have each other, even if they're not close to me."

Roxie's phone beeps and she lets out a sigh. I know that it means our time is almost up, but I'm not upset now that Roxie is going to tell her brother about us.

Slipping off my lap, Roxie leans forward to grab her shirt that I threw into the front passenger seat when a flash goes off.

"What was that?" She yells and covers herself up with her arm over her breasts.

"I'm not sure," I answer as I scan the area even though I have a pretty good idea. It's then I see someone in the parking lot beside one of the trees that line the park. "I think I see something. I'm going to go check it out. Stay here and lock the doors."

Tucking myself back in my pants as I get out, I head in the direction of the tree line. The closer I get, the more my heart rate picks up. There's someone standing there, and whoever it is seems to be waiting for me or doesn't care that I'm walking up on them.

"Who's there?" I call out.

"Just your friendly fellow Willow Bay student," a guy answers back. He doesn't say anything more until I get close enough to see it's that Jeremy guy from class.

What the hell is he doing here?

"I bet you're wondering why I'm standing here?" he smiles and waves his phone in the air.

"Something like that," I reply as I try to see what's on his phone screen. "Not many people come to the park at night."

"Oh, don't I know it. Only those who are trying to hide what they're doing," he cackles.

Does he know something, or is he just insinuating he does?

"Merrick, is everything okay over here?" Roxie quietly asks as she comes up from behind me.

"Everything's fine. Why didn't you stay in the car?" As she comes up beside me, I grab her wrist and pull her behind me. I don't want Jeremy to see her, even though I have a feeling it's already too late.

"Because you were gone too long," she yanks on her wrist, and I let go, not wanting to hurt her. "Jeremy?" She asks in surprise as she comes up beside me.

"Good evening, Ms. Hart. Sorry to interrupt your… night," he grins, letting us both know he is very much enjoying ruining our night.

"What are you doing here?" She asks, clutching my arm and then quickly letting go.

"Oh, I think the jig is up, Ms. Hart. I seem to have caught you at an inopportune moment—one I even got to capture with my camera." He wakes his phone up and turns it toward us. Right there on the screen is a picture of Roxie in the backseat of my car with only her skirt on.

"Really, Merrick, I don't know what you're thinking. Why bag the fat teacher when you could literally have any girl you want?"

Roxie shuffles behind me, and I hear her take in a strangled breath. I see red. Who the fuck is Jeremy to call Roxie fat? She's perfection.

"You need to shut your fucking mouth right now and

apologize before I slam your face into the pavement and give you a little makeover."

"You see, that's where you're wrong. I'm the one holding all the cards here. I have pictures of one of Willow Bay's teachers half-naked in a student's car. Don't you think the Dean would find it very interesting how that came to be?"

"Are you threatening me?" I growl and step closer, getting in his face.

Roxie grabs onto my arm and tries to pull me back, but I don't budge. I'm not letting this pencil dick threaten us.

"It's not a threat. It's a promise of what will happen if you don't give me what I want," he sneers.

"And what's that?" I have nothing to give to this guy. I'm a broke-ass college kid. It would be different if I drove some sweet-ass car that he caught us in, but no, if Jeremy had done his due diligence, he'd know by the way I live, I can't give him anything. The only thing I have or am close to having is my degree, and it's not like I can give it to him.

The right side of his mouth curls up. "Money, what else?"

"Sorry to break it to you, but unless you want my student loans, I've got nothing to give to you."

He laughs, and the picture of Roxie shirtless flashes for me again, nearly sending me over the edge. "It's not your money I want. It's hers."

"Jeremy," Roxie says softly. "I'm not sure if you're aware, but teachers here don't make a lot of money. At least I don't. I've only been here for two years, and—"

"I know *you* don't have any money, you stupid, fat cunt. It's your brother's I want. Why didn't you mention in class, he was a big deal?"

Unable to hold back any longer, I lunge for him. Pulling back my arm, I let go with everything I have in me and clock him in the cheek.

He goes down and stays down, much to my astonishment. I'm not a fighter, and I've never even punched anyone before.

"Oh my god, Merrick. What did you do?" Roxie shrieks from beside me as she tries to pull me away.

"He had it coming. No one should talk to you the way he did," I growl, circling him to see if he's going to get up.

"You need to leave. Now," she says urgently, pushing me toward my car. "Get out of here before he wakes up and calls the cops."

"So, what, I'm supposed to go home and wait for the cops to come to arrest me there?" I don't think so.

"I'll handle this," she continues to push me further away from the scene.

"I'm not leaving you here with him. Who knows what he'll do once he comes to."

"He won't hurt me if he thinks I'll give him money." Her hands come to rest on her hips. "Do you really think he found us here by accident?"

I hadn't thought about it before now, but it does seem strange.

"I'd bet my life he knew something was up and has been planning on doing something like this for a while. Now, go, and I'll call you later."

"I don't feel right leaving you here." I pull her body into mine and kiss the top of her head.

"I promise I'll be fine, but I need to handle this before you get kicked out of school with one semester to go, and I lose my job."

"Fuck," I yell. "I'm sorry. This is what you've been afraid of the whole fucking time, and here we are. I should have been more careful. I should have—"

"Stop, Merrick. I'm just as at fault as you are." Placing her hands on my chest, she leans up on her tip-toes and kisses me like it's the last time she'll ever taste me. It's hot and desperate and tragic. Pulling away, she starts to back up. "Go, please. I can't be worried about you *and* control this situation."

"Fuck," I growl out as I watch her walk back over to where Jeremy's on the ground. He's sitting up now and holding the side of his face while he watches us.

With one last backward glance, Roxie gives me a smile that breaks my heart. It says everything she didn't say.

It says goodbye before I even know there's an end to us.

17

It's been hours since I left Roxie in the parking lot with Jeremy. Each time I call her, I get her voicemail, and all of the fifty texts I've sent are unread.

The worst part is I don't even know if she's okay or not. Jeremy could have attacked her after I left, for all I know. I should have stayed and dealt with the consequences. Roxie shouldn't be the only one who has to deal with him. With each noise I hear, I jump up to check to see if it's the cops or Roxie.

Throwing myself down on my bed, I cover my face with my pillow and scream into it over and over again until my throat is hoarse. It does little to help the pent-up frustration that's coursing through my body.

Slowly, I sit up. Pulling up Roxie's number, I dial her knowing I'll get her voicemail again.

"Hello," she answers, her voice low and full of tears.

"Roxie? Why haven't you called me back?" I ask, barely more than a whisper. I'm not sure if it's because I can barely speak after screaming or because I'm afraid of what her answer will be.

"I… I had a lot to deal with." She sniffs and then clears her throat. "Everything's handled with Jeremy, so you shouldn't have to worry about him. If he bothers you, let me know, and I'll handle it."

I sit up against my headboard and close my eyes. "What did you do?"

"It doesn't matter now. What's done is done, but I need to go, Merrick," she chokes out.

"What aren't you telling me?" There has to be more. First of all, how did she get Jeremy to forget about what he saw? And second, why is she crying and trying to get off the phone with me?

"Not now, okay?"

"Then when? When can we meet up?"

"I don't know," she says so softly I barely hear her.

"I don't like the sound of that."

"Well, we don't always get what we want, now do we? Life isn't fair, Merrick, and it's about time you wake up and realize that," she angrily says, her tone sharp.

"I do know that, but you can't leave me hanging here. You won't give me any answers, and you're telling me you don't know when I'll be able to see you. Give me something."

She's quiet for a long moment, so quiet in fact that I pull my phone away and look to see if she's still on the line. "At least tell me, did you get him to delete the picture?"

"Yes, okay? I told you that you have nothing to worry about. Now enjoy the rest of your break."

Before I can respond back, she hangs up. I call her needing to know what the hell is going on, but when I do, it goes straight to voicemail. She's turned off her fucking phone.

Throwing my phone across the room, I hear it smash against the wall, but I don't care. Nothing matters until I talk to Roxie again.

18

TWO WEEKS LATER

Roxie's been avoiding me like the plague. She's gone so far as disconnecting her phone or getting a new number in an attempt to break our communication. I'm not sure which, and I don't know why. All I know is that a week ago when I tried to call her for the millionth time since the night Jeremy caught us, and she hung up on me, I got the message her phone has been disconnected or is no longer in service.

The only thing I can think of is that Jeremy demanded Roxie end all communication with me, or else he'd go to the Dean with the picture of her topless in my car and/or to the cops because I assaulted him.

Whatever it is, it isn't good. I'm not sure how Roxie's coping, but I've barely slept or eaten in the last two weeks. If school had been in session for these last two weeks, I'd be in trouble since I can't concentrate on anything for shit.

Tomorrow I'm getting answers, though. Classes are starting back up, and I'm going to wait for Roxie outside her office until

I talk to her. I don't care if I have to wait all day and all night. She's not going to be able to avoid me any longer.

Knowing I won't be able to sleep for another night, I pull up Roxie's Instagram. She hasn't posted anything new in the last two weeks, but I don't care. I miss her, and this is the only way I can look at her beautiful face since she wouldn't let me take any pictures of her.

I've even tried to find Jeremy on social media to see what he's been up to, but it's impossible since I have no idea what his last name is. It's not like he's going to spell out his nefarious ways on social media about how he wants to fuck over my life. I mean, he might, but that wouldn't be smart. I even asked my roommates if they know who he is and where he lives. Luckily for Jeremy, they have no clue who he is. Otherwise, I would have paid him a visit and kicked his ass all over again.

At some point, I must fall asleep while staring at pictures of Roxie and her brother since I wake up with my phone on my face, and it's dead. Plugging it in since it's both my clock and alarm, I hit the bathroom for a quick shower and to start my day of getting Roxie to talk to me.

After getting dressed, I have to wait for my phone to power back on. It's only then I see it's ten in the morning, and Roxie is probably already in class, which is perfect. I can wait outside her office until she has a break and finally get some answers.

Not wanting to waste any time, I drive the short distance to the science building and use the back entrance, putting me where the teachers' offices are on the first floor.

All the doors are closed, but when I get to Roxie's, I notice there's a piece of paper on the door saying she'll be gone for the week and classes will resume next week on Monday.

Is she seriously trying to avoid me and canceled her class for a week?

Unable to wait another week, I need to figure out some other way to get in touch with her. Somewhere at the school, they should have her address, but I have no idea how I'm going to convince anyone to give it to me. I'm sure that's as frowned upon as sleeping with your students.

Knowing she's going to be gone for the rest of the week, I decide I should probably go to my other two classes for the day. It won't do me any good to sit outside her door unless someone takes pity on me and calls her for me. I'm not going to resort to that tactic. At least not yet. While I'm in my classes, I can figure out a plan to get Roxie's home address or new phone number.

As I'm leaving the building, I notice the teacher's mailboxes across from the vacant secretary's desk. I search for Roxie's name and find it on the left side at the end. Looking both ways, I see no one around and pull out all of her mail. At first, it's just school memos and information about a facility lunch hosted by the science building, but then at the bottom of the stack, I find an envelope with her name and an address that isn't the school. It must be her house, and if it isn't, it may give me some clue as to where to find her. Taking a picture of the address with my phone, I put the mail back in her mailbox and leave the building, heading straight for my car.

Forget classes now that I might have a lead on where Roxie lives. I plug the address into my phone's GPS and head to Roxie's house—at least, I'm hoping it's her house. I don't plan on leaving until I get some answers. This has gone on for far too long.

It doesn't take me long to arrive in a nice neighborhood on the outskirts of town. The streets are lined with palm trees, and all the yards are neatly manicured. It gives off a quaint vibe that I like. It fits Roxie.

Pulling up outside an older Mediterranean-style house, I park along the street, even as I see no signs of life inside. That doesn't deter me, though. Nothing is going to get in my way of figuring out what the hell is going on. My only hope is this isn't someone else's house. That would be awkward, and I'm not sure how I'd explain myself.

Walking up the sidewalk, I take in the house before me. It's a little old, but damn, do I wonder how she can afford a place like this on a professor's salary at Willow Bay.

I ring the doorbell and step back. My gaze shoots from one window to the next, hoping to catch someone looking out or for any sign of moment. No one answers, so I ring and knock on the door this time. I almost give up and decide I'll wait in my car when the front door opens and the man I saw come out of her office months ago answers the door. He doesn't look happy. I'm not sure if it's because of me or he doesn't like being disturbed.

"Can I help you?" His voice is full of annoyance as his jaw clenches while he stares down at me.

Clearing my throat, I stand taller, not letting him see he's intimidating the hell out of me the longer he stares at me. "Is Roxie here?"

"Are you the fucker who's fucking up her life?" He growls and stands taller, blocking the entire entry.

"That's probably me, yeah. I didn't mean for anything bad to happen," I hang my head at the end. Never did I want any bad repercussions to affect Roxie for her getting involved in me.

"Yeah, well—"

He's cut off by Roxie pushing him to the side and then glaring up at him. "Let me handle this, Declan. It's my mess, and I need to clean it up."

"Oh, like the way you let me clean up mine," he darkly chuckles as he turns around and strides back into the house with a slight limp.

Closing her eyes, Roxie leans her forehead against the door and sighs. With her sigh, her entire body deflates. "What are you doing here, Merrick, and how the hell did you find me?"

"The 'how' doesn't matter, only that I did. Now, why don't you tell me why you've been dodging my texts and calls. Did you change your number?"

She doesn't look at me as she answers. "I'm doing it because it's what's for the best for the both of us. While you're a student at Willow Bay, I can't have any contact with you."

"Why? We can continue to keep meeting up in the library or your office. Parking lots are now out the question for obvious reasons."

"No, we can't, Merrick. I thought by now you'd get the picture that I…" she shakes her head and then nods at nothing in particular. "I can't be with you, plain and simple."

"Is this because of Jeremy? What did he do?" I step closer

and run the back of my knuckles along the soft skin of her cheek. "Did he threaten you?"

Roxie jerks away from my touch and looks around as if she's afraid someone is watching us. "What do you think happened?" She snaps. "Yes, he threatened me, and the only way to get rid of him was to pay him off with money I didn't have and had to ask my brother for. As you can imagine, he wasn't too happy to find out about you while I'm asking for thousands of dollars to pay off some asshole student of mine."

I'm sure he wasn't. I can't believe Jeremy blackmailed her.

"If I see Jeremy again, I'm going to pound his fucking face into the ground," I vow with my fists clenched at my sides. "Let me know how much your brother had to pay, and once I start working and get my bonus, I'll pay him back."

"It won't be enough, Merrick. Plus, Declan doesn't want your money. He just wants you to stay away from me."

I jerk back, feeling like I've been slapped in the face. My insides feel like they're being ripped out from my chest as I stare at her. I must have heard her wrong. "For how long?"

Her eyes turn glassy as she shakes her head. "I don't know. Right now, he's mad and threatening to leave and go back to Spain or some other country far away from me. You know I can't let that happen."

I do know, and I know there's no way in hell she's ever going to choose me. Not now. Not ever. It's always going to be her brother, not that I blame her.

Taking her hand in mine, I have to swallow the lump in my throat when I try to speak. "I know this," I gesture between her and me. "This was never serious for you, but it is, was, for me.

I've never been in love before, but if the way my heart is twisting and pounding in my chest while I feel like I'm dying inside is any indication of what it feels like when your heart breaks, then this is love."

It's the first time I've noticed she's not wearing makeup. Without her red lips and glasses, Roxie looks so much younger than she has every time I've seen her.

She chokes out my name as a tear slowly tracks down her cheek. When she opens her mouth, I press my finger to her lips.

I don't want to hear what she has to say. It will only make everything about this so much harder.

Dropping her hand, I try to smile, but I know I fail. Stepping back, I take her in one last time. From her bare feet up to her hips and the tank top that is barely holding in her large breasts. Breasts that I know my marks are now long gone from and will likely never wear my marks again. I take the longest look at her face. Her brown eyes drown me in sadness. Her face is pale, and there are dark circles under her eyes, making it look as if she's slept as little as I have since I last saw her.

"Have a good life, Roxie Hart. I hope you think of me fondly."

Roxie

"Stop fidgeting," I hiss at Declan.

"I can't help it. Crowds give me hives."

I turn and glare at him. "That's a load of bullshit, and you and I both know it. You used to play in front of thousands of people and ate up every minute the crowd cheered you on."

Leaning forward with his elbows on his knees, Declan hangs his head. "I'm not that guy anymore."

He isn't, and it kills me to see my once overly confident brother now shy away from the world. I only hope that with time he'll accept this new phase in his life and move on happily.

Taking his hand in both of mine, I squeeze it as we watch each student receive their diplomas.

"Are you sure you want to do this?" He asks after a few more students walk across the stage.

"More than anything. For the last four months, I haven't

been able to get his heartbroken look out of my dreams. I guess I should call them my nightmares."

Declan nods from beside me. "If I had known how you felt about him back then I—"

"You what? You wouldn't have paid off that little shit? You'd have let me sneak around with Merrick?" I whisper-yell, furious at what I've given up for the last few months. "What if he's found someone else?"

"If he's gone and fallen in love with someone else in this short period of time, then it was never meant to be."

"Easy for you to say. You and he can both have whoever you want," I snap.

"You give yourself too little credit, Rox. You can have anyone you want. Forget what all those kids used to say. You're beautiful inside and out, and any man would be lucky to have you."

"You're just saying that because I'm your sister. Most men don't like… my curves." I run my hand along the outline of my body.

"He did. Does," he corrects himself. "I saw the way he looked at you, and that boy thought you hung the moon. I can promise you he's not over you." He shakes his head and chuckles darkly. "And if you think I can have whoever I want, you're delusional. If I could have Dani back in my life…" he blows out a breath. "I'd do anything to get her back, but it's too late."

"Have you even tried to talk to her?" From what little I know, my brother shut her out of his life much the same way I did with Merrick and hasn't spoken to her since he got hurt.

"She doesn't need to worry about me. She still has another year of school and her soccer to think about. It wouldn't be right to put my baggage on her."

Wrapping my arm through his, I lay my head on his shoulder. "You're so much better now, though. You're getting around great, and the Blackhawks asked you to be their new assistant coach. You're not some guy who's lying around on my couch anymore. You've got a lot to offer if you just take that step."

I feel him kiss the top of my head. "Why don't we worry about your dating life for now and leave mine in the past where it belongs?"

Not wanting to fight with him, I keep any comments I want to say to myself. After this weekend, I'll go back to badgering him about his love life.

"I'm proud to announce this year's graduating class of...," the Dean drones on for another few minutes, and all I can think about is how I'm going to see Merrick up close and personal very soon.

Once the Dean finishes his speech, the students below cheer and throw their caps in the air.

The entire time I keep my eyes on Merrick. He doesn't cheer. He doesn't even look happy. I'm not sure why I brought Declan here. I thought it would be easy to find Merrick after the ceremony and tell him all the things I couldn't say the last time I saw him, but now I'm unsure of my plan. How will I find him in the sea of people below? He's not expecting me to be here, so he won't be looking for me.

"Hey, what's with the long face?" Declan asks, putting his arm around me.

"Why did I think I could do this? He could very well be gone by the time we get done there and passed everyone," I express my concerns as I watch what I'm guessing is Merrick's family come up and hug him.

"Text him and let him know you want to see him before he leaves," he says simply.

"He might not even see or feel the notification in time."

Grabbing my shoulders, Declan leans down until we're eye to eye. "Stop stalling and do something now before he leaves."

"I know, but—"

"Do you want him in your life or not?" I think he's annoyed I brought him along, and now I'm chickening out.

"I do," I turn to look back at Merrick and see he's weaving through the crowd like a man on a mission. What if he's headed for his new girlfriend? I want to close my eyes and avoid that train wreck.

"Hey, look, he's talking to his friend, and if you don't want to miss him, you better hurry up and get down there." Declan all but pushes me down the stairs. As my feet hit the floor, I look back to find my brother, only a foot behind me. He's in a button-up shirt with the sleeves rolled up to his elbows and a pair of dark-washed jeans. He looks good, and to see him be able to traverse the stairs easily brings a smile to my face. He's come a long way.

Turning back around, I try to push through the crowd to get to Merrick, but life's hard when you're short. No one seems to see me, and they can barely hear me over everyone talking.

Declan passes me and takes me by the hand as he pushes through the throng of people, not giving a shit if he pisses anyone off.

Dropping my hand, Declan moves to the side. Standing in front of me is Merrick. I take him in, what little I can with his gown hiding what's underneath. His brown hair is a little messy on the top from his cap, and he's grown out his usual five o'clock shadow into a trim beard that highlights his jawline. When I reach his brown eyes that are usually so full of life, I find them dull and lifeless.

I did this to him, and I don't know if I'll ever be able to fix the hurt I've caused him.

As if he can feel me looking him over, Merrick stops talking and looks my way. He shakes his head once and then rubs his eyes before shaking his head again.

"Roxie?" He questions disbelievingly.

"Hey, Merrick," I choke out. "Congratulations." I want to say more, but my words stick in my throat.

Merrick's friend nudges him with his elbow, which seems to bring him out of the stupor he's in.

"What are you doing here?" He steps closer but stops suddenly, his eyes trained onto something over my shoulder.

Unable to hold back, I close the remaining space between us and throw myself at him. Wrapping my arms around his waist, I bury my face into his chest and inhale his cedarwood scent. I thought I knew how much I missed him up until this moment, but I've been lying to myself. I can't stop the tears once they start, much to my embarrassment.

"Is she okay?" I hear someone ask.

Rough hands that I know belong to Declan try to pull me back, making me only cry harder. I don't want to leave. Not yet, when I have so much that I want to say.

"I've got her," Merrick rumbles, his arms wrapping around me. He shuffles us around, and the next thing I know, the sound of the crowd is gone, and it's only Merrick and me standing in a deserted hallway.

I look up at him to find his face creased with worry. I smile and wipe the tears from my face, knowing I probably look like a raccoon with mascara all over my face.

"I'm sorry," I utter, my fingers hovering over his face, wanting to smooth out his worry but holding back.

"What for?"

"I had no idea how powerful of an effect it would be to see you. I thought… I don't know what I thought except that I'd see if you'd talk to me and be willing to listen to what I have to say."

He pulls away, and my heart aches at the loss of him. Leaning against the wall, he crosses his arms over his chest. "Here's your chance. Talk." His words are clipped, and I understand he's mad. I'm mad, too—at both the time we lost and Jeremy blackmailing me—but when I look into his brown eyes, everything fades away.

"I was wrong about the way I handled things. I should have told you what was going on, but Declan—"

"Yes, your brother. I'm sure he didn't approve. Like I said before, I get my bonus in a couple of weeks, and I'll give it all to him. After that, you can let me know how much I owe you."

He's cold and detached, which I don't blame him for, even if he's never been this way with me. From the beginning, he's been open and carefree. I've done this to him, and it's my job to fix it.

"No, he didn't approve, but he's not the only reason I ended things. If we had kept seeing each other, Jeremy would have ruined both our lives."

"My life has felt pretty ruined since January. It's good to know you didn't feel the same," he bites out.

"I have, and I do, but I had to put our futures first and foremost. I should have told you that if you waited until today, we could be together, but I didn't want to hold you back."

"Hold me back," he laughs without humor. "How would you feel if the love of your life told you to take a hike?"

I gasp. He mentioned love back in January, but I thought it was just him being emotional at the time. I shouldn't have, though, because I knew then that I loved him.

"I'd be heartbroken. I have been heartbroken. The last four months have been some of the hardest months of my life. I wish I could turn back time and change things, but I can't. That's not how life works, but if you think that someday you'll be able to forgive me and want me back in your life, I'm here."

His face softens just the tiniest bit, and I think I may have broken through, but then his face hardens. "What about your brother? Will I still be a secret?"

Will the hurt from hiding our relationship from my brother be the end of us?

"He knows why I'm here."

"And does he approve?"

"You'll have to prove yourself to me, but I'm not going to

ask my sister to spend another day in misery just because I'm a miserable bastard," Declan says from behind me. How long has he been there?

"And what about Jeremy?"

"After today, he can't hurt you, and if he tries…" Declan cuts himself off. "Let's just say you don't need to worry."

Coming to stand beside me, Declan gives Merrick a once-over and then nods to himself. "I'm going to leave and give you two time to talk. I'll be home if you need me." Leaning down, he kisses me on the cheek. "Good luck."

I think I'm going to need it.

I watch as my brother walks down the hall and then out the door before I turn back to Merrick. He's looking at me with an unreadable expression on his face.

"I really am sorry, Merrick. I thought I was doing the right thing at the time." Tears fill my eyes as he continues to watch me with his stoically blank face.

He shifts against the wall, never taking his eyes off me. "You did the right thing, except you should have talked to me about it. The way you treated me made me feel like I was just some boy toy you used. All these months, I thought I meant nothing to you."

His words are my undoing. I can't hold back the tears that have been building with every word he speaks. "Nothing could be further from the truth. I only hope one day you'll be able to forgive me."

He takes a step toward me but stops. I'd give anything to be in his arms again. "And if I forgive you today?"

"Then I'll love you for the rest of my life. I won't let a single day go by where I don't tell you how much I love you," I cry.

His nostrils flare. "I never thought I'd hear you say you love me."

"I do, Merrick. I did for quite some time before everything blew up," I reach forward and take his hand. "I'm sorry I never told you. I let my insecurities get the better of me."

He shakes his head. "When are you going to start believing what I tell you?"

"Today. I'll start today. I promise." *If only you forgive me.*

"Don't cry, Roxie. I can't stand the thought of being the one making you cry." He opens his arms, and I don't waste any time diving into his arms.

Hugging him tightly, I rise up on my toes and kiss him. "I missed you."

"I missed you, too." Squeezing me, he pulls back to look down at me and chuckles. "I never thought today would end this way."

"What do you say we get out of here?"

A smile breaks out on his face. "Where do you want to go?"

"I have a graduation present for you that involves us going away for a couple of days if you can get away."

His eyes light up. "A weekend away?"

"I rented a cabin by Lake Arrowhead. All you have to do is pack a bag." I chew on the inside of my cheek, waiting for his reaction.

"What about your brother?" He nods in the direction Declan left.

"He's worked hard and is doing so much better. In fact, it was his idea for us to go away. Will you go away with me?"

"I'm sorry. I just—"

My heart falls to my stomach. It's over. "It's okay, I understand," I interrupt him, not wanting to hear an excuse.

Laying a finger over my mouth, he shushes me. "Let me speak, woman. I'll happily go away with you."

"You will?" I mumble against his finger.

"If you think I'm going to waste another moment away from you, you're out of your mind. If I wasn't dressed up under here, I'd be happy to leave right now."

"Really?" I happily cry out.

"Really. You have no idea how happy you've made me." A buzzing sound has him stepping back and fishing his phone out of his pocket. "Shit, that's Walker. He was who I was talking to before, and he's wondering if everything's okay. Can we go back out so that I can say goodbye to him? He has to get back to LA."

"Of course, we can. I'd never deny you your friends."

Merrick swoops down and kisses me, thrusting his tongue against mine and letting out a low moan. My fingers dance along the nape of his neck. I want to pull him closer, but he steps back before I have a chance.

Rubbing his thumb over my bottom lip, he smiles. "Don't pout. Let me go say goodbye to Walker, and then I'm all yours."

Hearing Merrick say he's all mine makes me beyond happy. I can't help the smile that stretches across my face.

Wrapping his arm around my shoulders, Merrick pulls me

close as he holds open the door for us to exit. "Come on, beautiful, let me introduce you to my best friend."

I snuggle into his side as we walk across the auditorium. The room isn't as crowded as it was before my breakdown. Wrapping my arm around his waist, I search the crowd for the man Merrick was previously talking to. He's not hard to find with his dark hair hanging down on his forehead, dark soulful eyes, and olive skin that I can tell is flawless from halfway across the room. He's tall with black jeans encasing his long legs with a black v-neck t-shirt that fits him like a glove. He exudes confidence.

The moment he sees Merrick, he cracks a bright smile that transforms him from a broody rocker to a handsome young man.

"Sorry to drag you back, but I wanted to say goodbye since you were such a baby the last time I left without seeing you," his friend pats him on the back.

"Fuck you, but thanks," Merrick laughs. "I can't help it if I'm a sentimental fool. One day you'll be too busy to even take my calls." His friend rolls his eyes and doesn't say anything. "Before you go, I want to introduce you to my girlfriend, Roxie. Roxie, this is my best friend and the lead singer of Crimson Heat, Walker Pierce."

I look up to see Merrick beaming.

"It's nice to meet you," Walker and I both say at the same time.

"It's about fucking time," Walker laughs. "And why the hell did you mention the band."

"Because she's been to see you play and… I don't know," Merrick shrugs. "I'm proud of you."

"This guy," Walker claps Merrick on the shoulder. "Has always been my biggest fan. If it wasn't for him and his belief in us, I'm not sure we'd be nearly as successful as we are."

That's so sweet. My heart melts at his words.

Walker lets out a sigh and looks around the room before his gaze comes back to Merrick. "Even though you're going to be a working stiff, don't be a stranger. Come visit when you can."

"I can say the same for you, and I expect my name and a plus one," he squeezes my arm. "And backstage passes to all of your shows."

"You tell Pen that, and if she agrees, you're on," Walker laughs. "No, but seriously, I'll make sure you have tickets to any show you want."

"Fuck, man," Merrick grabs Walker in a big hug and slaps him on the back. "I'm going to miss you."

"I don't know why he thinks I'm going to forget about him," Walker shakes his head. "I've known this guy since kindergarten. Kindergarten. And he magically thinks because I'm on the road—"

"And singing in front of hundreds of thousands of people with women throwing themselves at you night after night—"

"No, no," Walker looks around like someone might overhear. "Don't say shit like that."

Merrick only laughs. "Chill, dude, Pen isn't around. You're so easy to fuck with."

Walker wraps an arm around my shoulders and tries to pull me over to his side, but Merrick's arms go around my waist, and he pulls my back to his front, all while growling. "And he wonders why I might forget him."

I let them give each other shit for another few minutes, loving their friendship. It reminds me of Declan and me. Even though he's my younger brother, he's my best friend. The last year he's lived with me has been the hardest and yet the best year of my life.

Pulling my phone out of my purse, I shoot Declan a text letting him know I'm thinking about him.

Roxie: I love you, little D.

Declan: Please stop calling me that.
Everyone thinks I have a small penis,
when you say that.

I LAUGH, MAKING BOTH MERRICK AND WALKER LOOK AT me with curious looks on their faces.

"What's so funny?" Merrick asks.

"My brother's text. I'm sorry, I didn't mean to disturb you." My phone vibrates.

Declan: I love you too.
Is your weekend on?

Roxie: Yes, he's saying goodbye to his friend now.
I'll see you Monday.

A throat clears, getting my attention. When I look up, Walker smiles at me. "It was good meeting you, Roxie. I have a feeling I'll be seeing more of you."

"It was good to meet you too. I hope to be around for a long time, and I look forward to hearing more of your music."

Merrick links our fingers together.

Walker's phone lights up, and he frowns down at his phone. "I've gotta go, man, but I'm proud of you."

"Thanks, man," Merrick gives him a small smile.

With his hands down at his sides, Walker gives a low wave as he starts to walk away.

It's a sad moment. I think they realize how much life changes once you're finally out of school. If what I saw between them is anything to go by, I don't think they have to worry about growing apart. They'll be friends for life.

"Are you ready to go?" Merrick asks.

I don't answer him. Instead, I wrap him in a big hug and don't let go until he pulls away, letting him get what he needs in the moment.

"Thanks for that. Let's get out of here." He's quiet as we make our way through what's left of the crowd and outside into the heat.

Merrick peels off his robe and quickly removes his tie. "I'm not sure why we had to dress up when these damn robes hide everything."

"I don't know either."

"Where are you parked?" I point in the direction of my car. "Do you mind if we take your car to my house? I decided to walk instead of trying to find a parking place that's almost as far away as my house."

"Not at all," I tell him, not wanting him out of my sight for even a moment.

We're quiet as we make our way to my car. I'm not sure what he's thinking, but I'm running through everything to make sure I've taken care of everything for our weekend.

I spot my car and drag him along with me. I hit the button to unlock it and hear the chirp of the alarm turn off. Once inside, I turn the car on and blast the air conditioner to cool us both off. Before we leave, I run one finger along his arm and down to his hand. Merrick doesn't leave me hanging. Taking my hand in his, he smiles.

Turning, I cup his face with my other hand. "Are you okay?"

"Better than okay. I'm feeling all kinds of ways today. I feel like I lost one person while I gained another. In two weeks, I start my dream job, and I need to find a new place to live. It all feels like a dream."

"It's a lot for one day," I agree.

"To see you standing there today… it's a good day."

"I know you said you could, but if you can't go away this weekend, I'll understand. It's very last minute. If your family—"

"They already said their congratulations and goodbyes. The only plans I had for the weekend were to look for a place to live. I have to be out of my place by the end of the month. As soon as we get to my place and I pack a bag, we can start our life together."

I like the sound of that. Having a life with Merrick is not

something I ever let myself believe would happen, and now to know he still wants me after all this time only further assures me what we have is real. I bite the tip of my tongue to keep myself from asking him to move in with me and not bother looking at places. I hold back. Barely. Maybe I should see how we cohabitate with each other for the weekend before I mention it.

Not wanting to waste any more time, I put my car into reverse and back out of my parking spot. It doesn't take us long to get to Merrick's house. Cars line the road almost the entire way to his place. He was right not to bother driving.

This time when I step inside, the place isn't as neat and clean as it was before. In fact, it's downright disgusting as we walk side by side through the living room and down the hallway to his room. The place smells like pizza, stale beer, and dirty socks.

Opening his bedroom door, I'm met with a room that's clean and tidy. Even his bed is made, which is more than I can say about myself. I don't see the point when I'm going to sleep in it again.

I stay by the door and watch as he pulls a duffle bag out of his closet and starts throwing clothes in it. Kicking off his black dress shoes, he starts to undo his belt when he spots me. "You know you can come in and sit down."

"I know, but I think it's for the best if I stay where I am if we want to get there before dark."

I'm desperate to touch him and to have Merrick's hands on me, and I know if we start something, it will be hours before we come up for air. I can't take my eyes off him as he undresses in front of me, and each inch of his perfectly toned and tanned body is exposed to me. I grab onto the door handle to keep my balance.

"I like the way you think," he murmurs as if he can read my mind. "I'll be right back. Let me go grab me a few things from the bathroom, and then I'll be ready to hit the road."

FOUR HOURS LATER, WE PULL UP TO THE CABIN I RENTED for us. The sun is close to setting as we step out of the car and look at the cabin. It's small and cute with a wrap-around porch and a couple of rocking chairs. "Come on," I grab his hand and pull him up the steps. "It's small, but I thought it would be perfect for our first weekend getaway," I say as I put in the code on the door to unlock it.

"It's perfect. As long as there's a bed, I don't care about anything else."

Opening the door, we're met with a rustic living room and kitchen. The best part is the whole back of the cabin is windows, giving us the perfect view of the lake and the setting sun.

"Roxie, this is…"

"Beautiful," I supply for him. When he only nods, I pull him through the tiny area and out onto the deck that houses a hot tub. "What do you say we watch the sunset from in there?" My eyes flick to the hot tub even as I start to slip my sandals off.

Not wasting any time, Merrick grabs his t-shirt by the back

of the neck and pulls it off. Why is that move so insanely hot? Lifting my dress at the hem, I slowly pull it up and over my head. As I throw it on the deck, Merrick removes the rest of his clothes.

His long, thick cock is standing at attention, pointing straight at me, making me lick my lips.

"Fucking hell, you're perfection," he growls.

Reaching behind my back, I unclip my bra and slide the straps down my arms, letting it fall to the ground, all while never taking my eyes off the gorgeous man standing in front of me.

His eyes are darker than I've ever seen them before. I can tell from here he's breathing faster. He takes a step forward, and I think he's going to lunge for me and devour me, but instead, he throws off the cover to the hot tub. I watch as his back muscles and ass flex with the movement.

"The way you look at me drives me wild," he says as he starts slowly stroking his cock. "Now hurry up and take off your underwear before I rip them off."

I wouldn't be opposed to the idea, but I do as he asks and slide them over my hips and down my legs before I let them pool at my feet. Once I'm completely undressed, I'm rooted to the spot as I watch Merrick stroke himself.

He bites his bottom lip and moans. "What are you waiting for?"

"You're very distracting, Mr. Landry," I say as I step toward him.

"Let's see if I can help with that."

I watch as he gets into the hot tub and then holds his hand out to help me into the water.

The heat feels heavenly on my skin as I sink further into the water. Merrick glides me over to the side where we can look out at the water and the slowly setting sun.

"God, you're beautiful like this." His hands run over my shoulders and down my arms until he reaches my hands. Lacing our fingers together, he brings our hands above my head as he brings his front to my back. I can feel his erection probing my back, making me want to wiggle my ass against him, but I refrain. I don't want to ruin the moment when we so rarely got them in the past.

His hot breath skates along my jaw and down my neck before he places kisses along my shoulder.

"I forgot how good you smell," he nuzzles into my neck. Bringing our hands down around my front, he pulls my back to his front and holds me there. "This place is beautiful. Thank you for setting this up."

Turning my head, I look back at him. He looks down at me with a serene smile on his face. During these last few months, I never thought we'd be here, but seeing him now, I know we're going to be okay. "After how everything went down before, I wanted to show you how much you mean to me. I let my insecurities and fears rule me when I should have told you how I felt."

"I understand why you didn't. I was careless with how I didn't want to hide what we had from the world, but after Jeremy caught us, I realized how devastating it could be for both our lives. I still want to pay your brother back."

Turning back to the sun, I rest my head on his shoulder. "He doesn't want to be paid back. He only wants me to be happy."

"I promise to make you happy from today forward," he says, holding me tighter.

Four months ago, I wouldn't have believed it, but now I do. My eyes are open to how much this amazing man cares about me. I'm not an infatuation, but the woman he loves. I still can't believe he wants me, and now he's never going to get rid of me.

"I want to find a house on the bay to live in if the sunsets are anything like this," Merrick murmurs.

"They're even better," I state.

"Wait," he leans around to look me in the face. "Does your house back up to the bay?"

He's only been to my house once and never been inside, so I don't blame him for not knowing. I wish instead of hiding my relationship with Merrick from Declan, I would have told him before Jeremy blackmailed me. If I'd done that, then he'd know everything about me. But I know I can't live in the what-ifs. All we have is the here and now, and I plan to make the most of it.

"It does," I smile at him before pecking the corner of his mouth. "The view is the reason I bought a house in that crazy-expensive neighborhood." And the sunsets, but he'll see soon enough.

His brows furrow. "Why aren't we there then?"

"Because my brother is moving out of my house and into his new apartment as we speak. When we get back to Willow Bay, you'll have to watch the sunset with me." And maybe stay over.

"I like the sound of that." Resting his chin on my shoulder, he asks. "Are you going to be sad when he's gone?"

"Maybe a little bit, but we both need to live our lives, and neither one of us is going to do that while living together."

"Really? Does that mean—"

"There will be no more hiding for us, Merrick," I cut him off. "You can come to my house anytime you want. Spend the night—"

I'm cut off by being whirled around and his mouth crashing down on mine. Not wanting to waste another second, I wrap my arms around his neck and my legs around his trim waist. I use this position to start gliding up and down his shaft.

"Please tell me you're still on the pill," he moans against my lips.

Unable to speak, I nod while running my hands down his shoulders, along his ribs, and then the ridges of his abs until I'm met with his deep V.

He slides his hands up my outer thighs and grabs onto my ass, lifting me. Placing the tip of his cock at my entrance, I slowly take every inch of him until he's fully seated inside of me.

He's so big, and it's been so long, I feel almost too full. It's a delicious stretch that has me rocking back and forth as Merrick slowly moves in and out.

Skimming his lips along my collarbone and up the column of my neck, Merrick grips my ass tighter. "It's been too long. This is going to be fast and rough, but I promise I'll make it up to you later."

I don't tell him I don't care if it's fast or slow, rough or sweet. The way he makes my body sing with pleasure has me wanting him each and every way.

Merrick moves to sit down, making me straddle him as he thrusts up while using his grip to bring me down. He holds onto me so tightly that I know I'll have bruises tomorrow that I'll wear proudly.

Letting out a strangled groan, he stills inside of me. I'm so close, I continue to ride his thick cock as Merrick quakes underneath me. Heat explodes through my body, and stars fade in and out of my vision.

Merrick holds me tight against his chest as I come down, panting against his damp skin.

"I've dreamed of your tits, of this luscious ass, of being inside of your cunt, and in your heart," he kisses along my collarbone and down between my breasts until his lips are hovering over my heart.

With half-lidded eyes, I can't help but smile at his sweet words. When Merrick first came into my office, I never thought he would be the type to say such sweet words, but over the months we were together, and our time apart where I analyzed every conversation, I've learned there's so much more to this man that his dirty-talking mouth.

"You're in my heart as well. The months we've been apart, I've felt as if half of me was missing."

"And now?" He asks, nuzzling my neck.

"I've never been happier or felt so complete," I answer truthfully.

Standing with me in his arms, Merrick sits me on the side

of the hot tub. "I don't know about you, but I could use a little nap."

Now that he mentions it, I am tired. It's probably from the heat of the hot tub and the endless months of sleepless nights.

"A nap sounds good. I miss sleeping with you."

Merrick smiles down at me as he slips out of the hot tub and then helps me down. Lacing our fingers together, I let him lead me back inside the cabin and into the small bedroom with a beautiful view of the lake.

"This place really is great, and to know I get you all to myself for the entire weekend," he pulls back the covers for me.

"I feel the same way. It's long overdue, but it's the first of many weekends together," I say as I climb onto the bed, with Merrick following after me.

Lying behind me, Merrick curls around me and tangles our legs together. Nothing has ever felt as right as being in his arms. With each breath we take together as one, the more my body relaxes, and sleep takes over.

THE LIGHTEST OF TOUCHES runs along my arm and down my hip as I wake up. I smile, knowing it's Merrick, and turn over to find him resting on one elbow while he looks down at me.

"You're beautiful when you sleep, and you make these little noises—"

Horrified that I've been snoring while he's been laying here for who knows how long, I cover my face with my hands. "I wasn't snoring, was I?"

"No," he answers, peeling my hands away. "It's like little puffs of air. It's cute."

"It doesn't sound cute," I argue. Wanting to change the subject, I ask. "How long have you been awake?"

"Not long," he leans down and brushes his lips across mine. "I want to spend every weekend we can like this."

"Like what?" I ask for clarification. Turning on my side, I run my fingers along his arm to his shoulder and up to his neck. My thumb rubs across the scruff of his beard. I want to feel it between my legs.

"In bed with you and in our own private bubble away from the world."

"As often as you want, I'll let you in my bed. I know you'll be starting your job soon, but we can make time for each other. Plus, I'll have more free time for the next two months before school starts."

Rolling me onto my back, Merrick climbs on top of me and buries his face in my neck. "If I would have known you were coming back into my life, I would have told them I'd start in a month rather than two weeks. I figure two weeks is enough time to find a place to live and move in."

The thought of Merrick waking up somewhere else and not beside me twists my stomach into knots. Once school starts back, we won't have as much time to spend together.

Before I can think too much about it, I pull his mouth to mine and sweep my tongue inside. "Move in with me," I pant out when we finally break apart.

"Are you serious?" He pulls back while still hovering over me with wide eyes.

"Yes, I don't want to miss any more moments with you. I want to wake up to you every morning and go to sleep with you every night. Why should you look for a place when we are going to live together eventually anyway?" Or at least that's my hope.

"I… um… I'm speechless," he shakes his head. "I didn't mention apartment hunting because I wanted you to ask me to live with you."

"So you don't want to live together?" My heart falls to my stomach and then feels like it's being trampled on.

"I would love nothing more, but I don't want to push you for more than you're ready to give. I thought you wanted your house to yourself for a while."

"From my brother, not you, but if you want to wait, I'll wait. I know I don't deserve to have you back in my life so easily after what I put you through." Turning my head, I look out into the darkness, knowing I shouldn't have asked.

"Baby, don't be like that." Taking my chin between his thumb and forefinger, Merrick turns my face slowly to look back up at him. "If this is what you want, then I'll pack up all of my belongings and move in on Monday. Trust me; nothing would make me happier."

"Only if this is what you want. Don't do it for my benefit. I may have gotten ahead of myself." I knew I should have waited to see how the weekend went.

"No, I think you, no *we*, are right where we need to be." Kissing first the corner of my mouth, he moves to the other side and then places a soft kiss on the tip of my nose and then to each eye. "Ask me again."

I feel stupid, but I blow out a breath that makes his hair fall onto his forehead in a cute way that makes me smile. I don't want to miss moments like this with him because I am too chickenshit to ask again.

Instead of asking, I tell him what I want because that is what he deserves. "I don't want to miss any more moments with you. I want to be able to fall asleep in your arms and wake up to you between my legs."

His brow quirks up. "Is that the price of rent?"

"I think it's a fair trade given what you do to me."

He smirks as he scoots down the bed. "I'd like to make my first and last month's down payment now, then."

Merrick makes good on his promise. Each morning I wake up with a smile on my face as the man of my dreams brings me more pleasure with each passing day. And each day, I give it right back. Each night we get to know each other a little bit more, and I fall more in love with him each passing day.

When I first started working at Willow Bay University, I never thought I'd meet the man I was meant to spend the rest of my life with in my classroom, but life has a funny sense of humor.

Without chemistry, our love would be nothing.

ACKNOWLEDGMENTS

My family- your support means so much. Thank you for all of your encouragement and giving me the time to do what makes me happy.

To **my girls**: QB Tyler , Carmel Rhodes, Kelsey Cheyenne, Erica Marselas. I love each and every one of you. Thank you for all of your support.

Loni Ree: Thank you for bringing me on for the Love 101 collaboration. It's been so fun!

Wendy: I don't know what I'd do without you. Thank you for EVERYTHING you do!

Amanda: Thank you for talking me through when I didn't know where this story would go and being my cheerleader.

Thank you **Bex** for making my story into a book.

To all my **author friends**, you know who you are. Thank you for accepting me and making me feel welcome in this amazing community.

Lovers thank you for always being there day or night in my group.

To each and every **reader**, **reviewer**, and **blogger** - I would be nowhere without you. Thank you for taking a chance on an unknown author.

ABOUT HARLOW

Indie Author. Romance Writer. Reader. Mom. Wife. Dog Lover. Addicted to all things Happily Ever After and Amazon.

Harlow Layne is a hopeless romantic who writes sweet and sexy alpha males who will make you swoon.

Harlow wrote fanfiction for years before she decided to try her hand at a story that had been swimming in her head for years.

When Harlow's not writing you'll find her online shopping on Amazon, Facebook, or Instagram, reading, or hanging out with her family and two dogs.

ALSO BY HARLOW LAYNE

Fairlane Series - Small Town Romance

With Love, Alex - Women's Fiction, Self Discovery

Hollywood Redemption - Single Parent, Suspense

Unsteady in Love - Second Chance, Military

Kiss Me - Holiday, Insta-Love

Fearless to Love - Insta- Love

Love is Blind Series- Reverse Age Gap Romance

Intern - Office Romance

The Model - Workplace Romance

The Bosun - Military, First Responder

The Doctor - Raine's story - October 14

The Rocker - Coming February 17, 2022

Hidden Oasis Series

Walk the Line - First Responder, Suspense

Secret Admirer - Damsel in Distress, Opposites Attract, Suspense

Til Death Do Us Part - Accidental Marriage, Insta-love

You Make It Easy - MM, Second Chance

Collaborations

Basic Chemistry - Student/Teacher Romance - Sept 2

Forever - Student/Teacher, Curvy girl, enemies-to-lovers - October 8, 2021

Chance Encounter - MM, Enemies-to-Lovers - December 10

Worlds

Cocky Suit - RomCom, Office, Interracial

Risk - Forbidden, Sports

Affinity - Part of the Fairlane Series - Accidental Marriage, Enemies-to-Lovers